Remember Me 2
THE RETURN

Books by Christopher Pike

BURY ME DEEP
CHAIN LETTER 2: THE ANCIENT EVIL
DIE SOFTLY
THE ETERNAL ENEMY
FALL INTO DARKNESS
FINAL FRIENDS #1: THE PARTY
FINAL FRIENDS #2: THE DANCE
FINAL FRIENDS #3: THE GRADUATION
GIMME A KISS
THE IMMORTAL
LAST ACT
THE LAST VAMPIRE
MASTER OF MURDER
THE MIDNIGHT CLUB
MONSTER
REMEMBER ME
REMEMBER ME 2: THE RETURN
ROAD TO NOWHERE
SCAVENGER HUNT
SEE YOU LATER
SPELLBOUND
WHISPER OF DEATH
THE WICKED HEART
WITCH

Available from ARCHWAY Paperbacks

Christopher PIKE

Remember Me 2
THE RETURN

AN ARCHWAY HARDCOVER
Published by POCKET BOOKS
New York   London   Toronto   Sydney   Tokyo   Singapore

AN ARCHWAY HARDCOVER

 An Archway Hardcover published by
POCKET BOOKS, a division of Simon & Schuster Inc.
1230 Avenue of the Americas, New York, NY 10020

Library of Congress Catalog Card Number: 94-66301

ISBN: 0-671-87257-5

First Archway Hardcover printing September 1994

10 9 8 7 6 5 4 3 2 1

AN ARCHWAY HARDCOVER is a trademark of Simon & Schuster Inc. The colophon is a registered trademark of Simon & Schuster Inc.

Printed in the U.S.A.

For all the Wanderers of the world.
May they one day remember where they came from.

Remember Me 2
THE RETURN

CHAPTER
I

*J*EAN RODRIGUES did not want to become her mother. A not quite forty-year-old woman with five kids, a dead husband lost to booze, working sixty hours a week at a coffee shop just to pay the rent on a rundown house in the wrong part of town and to put food in the mouths of children who could not have cared less about her. Most of the time Jean couldn't give a damn, not about school or work or even about herself. Yet sometimes she'd watch her mother as the woman got dressed for work, the lines of ruined dreams on her weary face, and Jean would feel sorry for her. She'd think, There must be something that would make my mother smile. There must be more to life than what I see waiting for me. Yet Jean could never see that "more," and so she seldom smiled herself.

Jean Rodrigues was eighteen years old and it was two weeks before her high school graduation. Her father had been Mexican, pure Aztec—at least that's what she was told. Her memories of him were few; he had died of pneumonia and heart failure while she was still in first grade. Her mother—she wasn't positive what her mother was. Half Hispanic, a quarter Italian, two-thirds the rest of the world. The numbers and genes never added up. Jean supposed the same was true for her. But Jean knew she looked good, no matter what her gene pool or how broke she was. Her long dark hair was her glory. She wore it unadorned and straight down to her butt and washed it every night with an herbal shampoo—one of the few luxuries she allowed herself. Her face was strong; relatives said she took after her father. Her nose was big, but since her mouth was as well, the flaw only enhanced her beauty. She may have had her father's fearless expression, but she had her mother's body. They were both voluptuous. Her looks were one of the things Jean felt good about. There were so few things.

That evening was a warm Friday. If Jean had read the papers closely and had an excellent memory, she would have remembered it was exactly fifty-two Fridays after the death of another eighteen-year-old in another section of Los Angeles, a certain Shari Cooper. Like Shari of a year ago, Jean was in her bathroom preparing to spend Friday night at a birthday party for a friend. Her friend was Lenny Mandez. Jean had been dating Lenny for about three months and had a special surprise for him tonight. It was so special that she wondered if she should let him know about it on a night reserved for celebration. She was six weeks pregnant with his kid.

My mother got pregnant with me when she was eighteen. The same sad story, all over again. I don't want to become my mother.

Jean knew why she was pregnant, besides the obvious reason that she'd had sex. Six weeks earlier when Lenny and she had made love, their condom had broken. And there they were being so responsible, practicing safe sex and all. She'd been a fool to believe all that hype, she thought. The only hundred percent safe sex was between Barbie and Ken, and she'd heard rumors they weren't doing it anymore. What made it worse was that she wasn't sure if Lenny knew how badly things had misfired that night. She worried that he might think the kid belonged to someone else. But it wasn't a huge worry—Lenny was cool—not as huge as the kid growing inside her. She didn't know what to do. She didn't want to think about it, so she planned to get loaded that night.

Jean was brushing her hair when the car horn outside startled her, although she'd been waiting for it to sound. Her best friend, Carol Dazmin, was driving her to the party. Jean did not have a car. She did work after school and most weekends at a Subway Sandwich but only to supplement her mother's meager income and to buy clothes and pot. Not for a car. Jean smoked pot practically every day; it was the only thing that made the clocks on the walls at school fun to watch. Carol got loaded with her, too, but spent her days staring at the other girls. Carol was a lesbian, but she never hit on Jean or anything and it was OK. In fact, Carol was another of the few things in Jean's life that could be called positive. Carol was one of the kindest and funniest people Jean had ever met.

At the sound of the horn, Jean jerked her hand the wrong way and ended up breaking the handle off her brush with it right in her hair. Even if she'd possessed a perfect memory and had read every paper in town, Jean wouldn't have known that Shari Cooper had broken brushes regularly. Jean stared at the plastic handle in her hand before pulling the clump of bristles from her hair. She had never broken a brush before.

Jean left the bathroom and walked into the living room. It was getting dark, but her younger stepbrothers and -sisters were still outside playing, even four-year-old Teddy. The only one Jean really felt close to was Teddy; the world had yet to ruin him. As for the rest, she didn't care if they ever came inside. Her mother had crashed on the couch in front of an old "Star Trek" rerun on TV. Jean had no interest in science fiction or anything to do with space. She would just as soon the government spent the money on nuclear bombs.

"Hey, *Mamá,*" Jean said softly, staring down at her mother. "I'm knocked up. Knocked up and dropped down."

Her mother stirred. Her hair was already gray; she couldn't be bothered dying it. She had on green coffee-stained pants, a white blouse she had worn the past two days. Her lipstick was a cheap color; it looked as if she'd put it on in front of a dusty windshield rather than a clean mirror. Most of all she looked tired. She had to be up at four to be at work on time. Jean felt that somehow she was standing before a mirror as she studied her.

Her mother yawned. "Did you say something, Jean?"

Jean hesitated. She'd have to tell her sometime. Or would she? Maybe Lenny would talk her into an abortion. Or perhaps he'd just take her out and shoot her. There were all kinds of possibilities, when she thought about it.

"No," Jean said. "I'm going out."

Her mother opened her eyes. "Where are you going?"

"Lenny's having a party. It's at his house."

"Will his parents be there?"

"His parents are dead, Mom. I told you that."

"Well, who will be there? Just you kids and a cloud of smoke?"

Jean acted bored. "Mom, nothing like that's going to happen."

Her mother snorted. "Yeah, like it doesn't happen every day. What do you take me for, *mija?* One of your teachers at school?"

"I don't know."

"What time are you coming home?"

"Midnight, maybe a little later."

"Don't you have work tomorrow?"

"Yeah. I'll be there. Do I ever miss?"

Her mother shook her head. "I don't know what you do anymore, Jean. Except that you don't stay around here much. What's this Lenny like? Have I met him?"

"You met him last week."

She scratched her head. "He wasn't that black fella, was he?"

"Mom! He's the same color as you and me. He's a great guy. I like him. It's his birthday tonight."

Her mother nodded. She liked birthdays. They were next to All Saints days in her book. "What'd you get him?" her mother asked.

Jean had passed the two-minute-get-your-ass-in-gear mark. Carol honked again. Jean stepped toward the door, saying, "I got him something special. I'll tell you about it later. Don't worry if I'm a little late."

"If you don't come home, I'll worry," her mother called after her.

Jean opened the door and stepped outside the house, the same house she'd lived in all her life. She drew in a deep breath of smog. North and south, east and west, her neighborhood was in the throes of a holocaust. Had been since the word *ghetto* was first used.

"I wouldn't," Jean muttered under her breath.

Carol had made herself up, much more than Jean had. Carol had on a tight black leather skirt, a long-sleeved red blouse, fake silver and gold chains. Jean wore blue jeans and a yellow shirt. Carol was not butch; she liked to attract the girls as a girl. Jean knew Carol's fantasy, Darlene Sanchez, would be at the party. Jean also knew Carol was wasting her time on Darlene, who needed guys the way a smoking car needs a quart of oil.

But Darlene was not in a romantic mood these days. Her boyfriend, Sporty Quinones, had been gunned down near the projects in a drive-by only two weeks ago. Lenny had been with him at the time, but hadn't been hurt. Sporty had taken three shots in the chest and bled to death in Lenny's hands. At the funeral Darlene had not been silent in her mourning; there was too much fire in her blood. Even as they lowered Sporty into the ground, she shouted for vengeance. That was the trouble with drive-by hits; they were just guns poked out of dark windows. The killers didn't leave cards. Darlene said she knew who did it. Lenny didn't know how; he said he didn't even see the car. The whole thing confused Jean. She didn't know what the hell the guys were doing so close to the projects in the middle of the night. That was like walking into a sewer pipe and asking not to get dirtied. She missed Sporty as well; he had been a good friend. If it hadn't been for Lenny, she might have gone out with him. They had fooled around a little at some boring party just before Lenny and she got together.

"Guess what?" Carol said as Jean climbed into the car. Carol had a ten-year-old red Camaro that had once been hit by a school bus. It sounded like a tank under enemy fire, but it always started, which was the important thing.

"What?" Jean said, closing the car door.

"You have to guess." Carol put the car in gear and they rolled forward.

"I don't want to guess."

"I got asked out today."

"Who asked you out?" Jean asked.

"You know the guy with the Russian accent at the McDonald's on Herald?"

"That guy? His face is scarred."

Carol giggled; she often did. Her lips were glossy, her eyelids neon. She was skinny as a wire plugged into a shorted socket. She had a lot of energy. She could eat two Big Macs with fries at lunch break and still do situps in P.E. an hour later. She was pure Hispanic but wore so much white powder that she looked as if she were auditioning for a circus clown.

"What do you think?" Carol asked.

"About his scars?"

"No! About him asking me out. He knows I'm a lesbian, and he still wants to go out with me. Doesn't that make him some kind of pervert?"

"No. I bet he thinks he can turn you on. Are you going out with him?"

"I don't know. I told him to come to the party tonight. Do you think he'll come?"

"Why do you keep asking me questions like that? I don't even know the guy."

Carol nodded excitedly. "I hope he comes. It might make Darlene jealous."

"I wouldn't count on it."

Carol lost her smile. "Don't you think she likes me—just a little? And don't say you can't answer because you don't know her."

"Yes. I think Darlene likes you. I just don't think she wants to sleep with you. God, Carol, the girl is a complete horn dog. She's slept with just about every guy at school."

"Yeah. But she's just suffered a major personal loss. That can sometimes shake up a person's sexuality. I heard that on 'Oprah.' There was a woman on there who didn't become a lesbian until her husband's head was cut off by a helicopter blade."

Jean groaned. "Oh, brother."

"What is it?"

"I need some *mota.* Do you have a joint?"

"At home, not with me. But there'll be plenty of stuff at the party. Can't you wait?"

"I suppose."

"What's bothering you, Jean? You look like you're worried about your sexuality."

"I'm pregnant."

"*Qué?*"

"I'm pregnant."

Carol almost rammed the back of a bus. "Wow! That's big. Whose is it?"

Jean was disgusted. "What do you mean, whose is it? It's Lenny's. He's my boyfriend. What kind of question is that?"

"I was just asking. I just wanted to be sure. Wow. What are you going to do?"

"I don't know. What do you think I should do?"

"I don't know. Get rid of it."

Jean shook her head. "Just like that? I don't know if I can do that."

"Have you told him?"

"I was thinking of telling him tonight."

"That should liven up his party."

"Shut up. Maybe I'll tell him later. I haven't even told my mom yet."

"Don't tell your mom. She won't let you go out anymore."

"I'll think about it," Jean said.

"What did you get Lenny for his birthday? I got him a book."

"What kind of book?"

"I don't know. It had a scary cover on it. Does Lenny like scary stuff?"

"I don't think he's read a book in his life. I don't know if he can read."

Carol laughed. "I was thinking the same thing! I was thinking this is the stupidest present I could possibly buy him! That's why I bought it. What did you get him?"

"Nothing so far. Let's stop at the record store. Maybe I can buy him a tape."

Carol settled back down. She reached over and touched Jean on the leg. Her voice came out gentle. Jean knew Carol was not as insensitive as she liked to pretend.

"If you do keep the baby, then we could all play with it," she said. "It might not be so bad. It might even be fun."

Jean sighed. "Nothing's fun anymore."

CHAPTER

II

*L*ENNY MANDEZ had a hilltop home with a view. Unfortunately, the house rested on a weed-choked plot of land between a slum and a ghetto. The surrounding area was covered with aged oil wells that creaked so badly in the middle of the night it sounded as if the house were under attack from an army of arthritic robots. The latest earthquake had actually made some of his neighbors' homes stand up straighter. The whole area looked as if it had been thrown together for the express purpose of violating every code in the book. Lenny's home had two bedrooms for the cockroaches and a bathroom for the real nasty creatures. Still, it wasn't a bad place to have a party, Jean thought, as long as there was enough booze and dope. Fortunately, that was never a problem with Lenny. Intoxicants followed him the way ants beat a path to the food across his kitchen floor.

Lenny Mandez was twenty, but if his age was measured by mileage rather than years, he was ready for retirement. He had joined his first gang while walking home from kindergarten. He was in juvenile hall for stealing a car he didn't know how to drive when he was thirteen. But that two-year stint inside sobered him some, and Lenny returned to public school and graduated from high school last year. He had a full-time job now, working as a mechanic at a gas station owned by an uncle. He owed allegiance to no particular gang, but had friends in all the wrong places and made as much money dealing drugs as he did tuning engines. Jean knew he was trouble, she was no fool, but she took solace in the fact that he didn't like being a pusher, anymore than he liked the idea of returning to prison. He told her that he was trying to change, and she could see that he was. He took a couple of night classes at the city college—general ed stuff. He didn't know what he wanted to do with his life any more than she did. They had that in common, at least.

She had met him through the late Sporty Quinones, who, at the age of twenty, had still been trying to get a high school diploma. They had been introduced in the middle of the street, literally, and for a moment, when she'd looked into his dark eyes, she forgot about the oncoming cars. There was passion in his eyes, she sensed, as well as danger. She wondered if that's what it took to turn her on—the possibility of a bad end. He had a great body; she had seen a few in her day. He had heavy muscles, generous lips, and wore his straight black hair long onto his shoulders. He had taken a hip tone with her. "Hey, baby, I heard about you. Heard you were hot. What do you say we get together tonight?" Of course she had told him where to stick it, and he had laughed, reverting to a more subdued tone, which she was to learn was more normal for him. He had taken her to the movies that night, and they had necked so hard in the back row they had turned a PG Disney film into a hard R erotic mystery. That was what she liked most about Lenny —the mystery. Even after six weeks of dating, she still had no idea what he was thinking. At Sporty's funeral, as his best friend was lowered into the ground, he hadn't changed the expression on his face. He could have been staring at the sky for all the emotion he showed.

Jean ended up getting Lenny a Los Lobos tape, which he slipped into the boom box as soon as she and Carol arrived at his house, and cranked up the volume. Jean assumed that meant he liked it even though she hadn't had a chance to wrap it. He gave her a quick kiss and handed her a beer and she sat on the couch in the living room with a bunch of people she hardly knew and the party moved forward as they always did. There was alcohol, pot, music, laughter, and cursing. She and Carol cornered a hookah loaded with Colombian Gold near the start of the festivities and each took four hits so deep into their lungs that they could feel their brain cells leaving on the sweet cloud of smoke as they exhaled. They both began to laugh and didn't stop until they remembered they had nothing to laugh about, which was an hour later. So the first part of the party passed painlessly.

Even though Jean got loaded regularly, marijuana often had an undesirable side effect on her psychology. The moment her high began to falter, her mood sometimes plunged, so rapidly that she felt as if she were sinking into a black well. In other words, the pot bummed her out as surely as it made her laugh, and this was one of those unfortunate times when, after an hour of giggling, she felt close to tears. But since she seldom cried, and never in front of other people, she just got real quiet and tried not to think. She didn't want to know she was in a place she didn't want to be with people she didn't care about and who didn't care about her. That her whole life was headed in the wrong direction and that it wasn't going to change because that was just the way the world was. That she was pregnant and didn't want a baby and didn't want to have an abortion and didn't want to end up like her mother. It was this last thought, spinning around in her head, that caused her the most grief. And the weird thing was, her mother was one of the few people in her life she actually respected.

Come midnight, though, when the party began to thin out, and the dope began to filter from her bloodstream, her depression lifted sufficiently so that she was able to talk again. At the time she happened to be sitting on the end of Lenny's bed watching as Darlene Sanchez used the cracked mirror precariously attached to the top Lenny's chest of drawers to replait a few loose braids. Darlene was Hispanic, but wanted to be black; a formidable task, to be sure, since she was naturally whiter than Carol after makeup. Sporty Quinones had been Darlene's first non–African-American boyfriend, a fact that was somewhat at odds with her reputation of having slept with most of the juniors and seniors in the school. But who was counting, colors or numbers. Darlene was hot, no debating that.

"How are you feeling, girl?" Darlene asked, gazing at her in the mirror.

"I'm all right," Jean said.

"You looked like hell all night."

"Thanks a lot."

"No, I mean your mood." Darlene lifted a few strands of hair above her head and, in the blink of an eye, braided them. Her braids made her look pretty scary when she wore them just right. Her long painted fingernails were just as bad. They reminded Jean of razors dipped in blood. Darlene added, "You look like someone just died."

Jean realized she had a can of beer in her hand and took a sip. "Someone just did."

Darlene acted pissed. "Great! You had to bring that up. I'm here to have a good time, and you have to talk about Sporty."

"I wasn't talking about him." Jean shrugged. "In this town someone dies practically every hour."

"Yeah, right. God, what a downer you are."

Jean burped. "Sorry."

Darlene waved her hand. "It doesn't matter. I don't mind talking about him. We're going to talk about him later anyway. We're going to have a little meeting when the party's over, Lenny and I. You should stay for it."

"What kind of meeting?" Jean asked.

"You'll see."

"I came with Carol. Can she be there?"

Darlene seemed exasperated. She could change her

expression quicker than most people inhaled. "That girl. She doesn't know what she is. Do you know what she said to me this evening?"

"I can guess."

"She said, 'You know, Darlene, there are two sides to everything. You don't know what belongs on front until you check the behind.' Can you believe she said that to me?"

"I don't even know what it means."

"It means, dope head, that she's still trying to get in my pants. Lenny tells me you're straight as an arrow. How can you have a dyke as a best friend?"

"It's easy. She's not a dyke to me. She's a great girl."

Darlene paused. "Have you two ever done it?"

"Done what?"

"Had sex, for godssakes! Have you?"

"No. Carol's not interested in me that way."

"What is she interested in then?"

"She's my friend. She needs friends as much as straight people. Maybe more. Maybe you should try being her friend rather than always badmouthing her."

"Maybe she should quit hitting on me first," Darlene said.

"She's not hitting on you. She's just flirting with you. You should be flattered."

"I'm not. She makes me nervous. She makes me feel like I might be a *joto* and not know it."

"Maybe you are a *joto,* Darlene." Jean allowed herself a rare smile. "Anybody who goes around with a head looking like a snake fest has got to have something wrong with her."

Darlene laughed. "Hell, you're probably right." She

finished with her hair and turned around. "How do I look?"

"Am I the right person to ask? I just told you. You look great."

"Thanks. You want to go get something to eat?"

"You mean, leave the party?" Jean asked.

"Yeah, I mean leave the party. You can't eat any of the rot in Lenny's refrigerator. We can hit the Jack-in-the-Box down the street and be back in twenty minutes."

Jean shook her head. "You go ahead. I don't feel very hungry."

Darlene sat on the bed beside her friend, concerned. "Really, are you all right, Jean?"

Jean shrugged. "Yeah, I'm just tired."

"Are you and Lenny getting on all right?"

"Yeah." Jean paused. "I think so. Do you know something I don't?"

Darlene hesitated. "No." She stood quickly. "I'll be back soon. Remember that meeting. I want you there."

"I won't be there unless Carol's there. She's my ride home."

"Aren't you going to spend the night with Lenny? It is his birthday, after all."

"No," Jean said. "My mother would freak."

Darlene seemed to think for a moment, then nodded. "That's what mothers are for."

Darlene left. Jean continued to sit on the edge of the bed and sip her beer. She studied herself in the mirror. It was only then she remembered the dream she'd had that morning. It had been wonderful yet simple, painful to wake from. She dreamed she was floating above her house and that just a few blocks away she could see a colorful amusement park, the rainbow of shimmering lights illumining her insides as much as the neighborhood. The feelings of the dream had been more important than the actual events. She knew that if she would just fly over there, she could enter that place of constant fun and excitement. Where there were people who cared and things to do that meant something. And in the dream she was being given that choice, to leave her house, her life, and never return. Why had she awakened? She sure as hell hadn't said no to the offer. Now the memory of the dream made her sad. Made her sad that it was gone, forever.

After some time Lenny entered his bedroom. He had on his black leather jacket; he seldom took it off, even on nights as warm as this. His long black hair was pulled back in a ponytail. They had talked little all night. Conversation wasn't big with either of them. They were better just sitting and watching a movie together, or smoking a joint, or making love. She had assumed they'd have sex tonight since, as Darlene said, it was his birthday. But now she had to wonder if she could talk herself into the right mood. Lenny sat on the bed beside her and leaned over to give her a kiss. She kissed him back—sort of. He sensed her lack of enthusiasm and drew away.

"What's wrong?" he asked.

"Nothing." She touched his leg. "How are you doing?"

"Good. Great party, huh?"

"Yeah. That was great dope. Where did you get it?"

He shrugged. "The usual sources. Where did Darlene go?"

"To Jack-in-the-Box. She was hungry."

"We have pizza in the living room," Lenny said.

Jean forced a smile. "It's on the living room floor. I think Darlene worries about hygiene."

Lenny chuckled; it sounded forced as well. "Then I don't know what she was doing with Sporty. That guy had equipment that needed to be machined to get clean."

"Was he that bad?"

Lenny paused and stared at her. "I don't know. He just told me so many stories."

"About so many girls?"

Lenny nodded. "Yeah. You must have seen how he carried on at school?"

"Yeah, he got around some, I guess. When Darlene wasn't around."

"But they weren't going out that long," Lenny said.

"Really? I thought it was a few months."

Lenny continued to watch her. "Something's bothering you, Jean. What is it?"

She lowered her head. "Well, there is something I wanted to tell you. I should have told you earlier, but I was afraid. But I don't know if this is the right time, either."

Lenny sucked in a deep breath and became still. She sensed his rigidity more than saw it because she continued to keep her head low. Finally he let the breath out.

"Yes?" he said softly.

"I'm pregnant."

The two words seemed to float out of her mouth and into a vacuum. The room became a bowl sitting on some troll's table, and they were breakfast. She raised her head and saw that Lenny had closed his eyes. A vein pulsed on his forehead. It looked as if it might pop if the pressure wasn't released soon. She wanted to say something to make him feel better like I'll get rid of it or maybe the test kit was wrong. But she doubted he would have heard her at that moment. His mind seemed to have fled to a place where there were no words. Finally, though, he opened his eyes and looked at her. His expression was strangely blank.

"Are you sure?" he asked softly.

"Yes." She paused. "I'm sorry. Lousy birthday present, huh?"

"I've had better. What do you want to do?"

"I don't know. What do you want to do?"

"It's up to you."

"No, it's up to both of us." She felt a painful lump in her throat. She had taken her hand off his leg, and she wanted to put it back, to hug him, maybe kiss him again. But they were like two strangers sitting in a cheap motel room. At least that was how the two people in the cracked mirror looked. Jean regretted having started the conversation in front of their reflections. It made her feel more lost. How did she really feel about Lenny? She had told him she loved him; he had told her the same. But those were just words. She didn't believe she could love him because she didn't know what love was. She didn't even know if there was such a thing, if it wasn't all hype. She added, "We can keep it or we can get rid of it. I'm not going to force it on you."

"How much does an abortion cost?" he asked.

"Three hundred dollars. About."

He smiled thinly and shook his head. "That's

mucha lana. You were raised Catholic. Could you go through with an abortion?"

She sighed. "I don't know." His next question caught her off guard.

"What do you think he'd look like?" he asked.

She hesitated. *"Bueno.* Like the two of us. But it might be a she, you know."

"Have you ever seen pictures of me when I was a baby?"

"No. You haven't shown me any." She paused. "I'd like to see some."

"No, you wouldn't. I looked awful. But maybe he would look—better." He stood and eyed the door. "Let's talk about this later when no one's around. Right now I have to enjoy my twentieth birthday party. It's the only one I'm ever going to have."

"Lo siento, I'm sorry," she said again.

"Don't be sorry," he said as he left the room.

Ninety minutes later Jean was sitting in the living room with Lenny, Carol, and Darlene. After Lenny had left her, Jean had fallen back on the bed and passed out for an hour. She hadn't dreamed, only entered a black void where there was no sound or feeling and slept the sleep of the dead. She didn't even know who she was when she awakened in the dark. The disorientation had lingered. Who had turned off the bedroom light? She didn't know and it didn't matter.

The four of them were the only ones left at the party. Jean sat on the couch with Lenny. Carol was on the floor, acting bored. Her Russian boyfriend had never shown. Darlene, as usual, paced. Darlene wanted revenge, she wanted blood. Her little meeting was about planning a hit on Sporty's murderers, specifically on Juan Chiato. Juan was the biggest drug dealer at their high school, although he hadn't been to class in ten years. He was twenty-one years old, high up in the Red Blades, one of the most vicious of the inner city gangs. Jean knew Juan by sight; she had met him twice at Lenny's house. He'd been leaving as she went in. Out of necessity, Lenny said he occasionally had to deal with Juan, although Lenny clearly did not like to be in the same room as Juan, who was known for his violent temper. But Juan had direct contact with Colombian drug lords and practically set the price of cocaine in their neighborhood. His face was badly scarred from knife fights. Jean thought he looked like one of Satan's first lieutenants. She hadn't known Sporty was connected to Juan, but she supposed she'd been mistaken.

"Let me tell you why I know it was Juan," Darlene said as she strode back and forth in front of them, a cigarette in her hand. "The week before Sporty died, he told me about a deal he had going with Juan. You didn't know about it, Lenny. Sporty told me Juan had sworn him to secrecy. Anyway, Sporty told me about it because he could never keep his mouth shut when he was drunk. It had nothing to do with drugs. Juan had stolen a truckload of Levi's jeans. He had slipped onto a freight company's lot with a gun and put the barrel to the security guard's head and driven away with the trailer. He wanted to use Sporty to sell the jeans to certain stores. Sporty was game. The commission looked good, and he thought dealing with store owners would be a lot more pleasant than the jerks that hung around Juan. But what he didn't know was that Juan was just using him. The stores he sent Sporty to paid protection to the Bald Caps. You know them?"

Lenny nodded. *"Cierto.* They're a small gang, but they control much of downtown, especially around the convention center and the skyscrapers. Why did Juan want to piss them off?"

"I asked Sporty that," Darlene said. "He thought maybe Juan was trying to set something up between the Red Blades and the Bald Caps. Juan was trying to move up in the Blades, and he was impatient. He wanted some action that he could lead, show the others how strong he was. He wanted a fight. He sent Sporty out, not to sell jeans, but to start a war with the Bald Caps. Right away Sporty ran into trouble. The Caps cornered him and threatened to cut out his heart for daring to enter their territory. They stole his van full of jeans. Sporty went running back to Juan and told him what had happened, but Juan didn't want to hear about it. He gave Sporty an ultimatum—either he got the jeans back or *he* was going to cut out his heart. Sporty yelled at him, said he had just been set up. Then Sporty made a big mistake. He told Juan he was thinking of going to the police to tell them the whole story."

"No," Lenny said, shaking his head. "He wouldn't have been that *estúpido."*

Darlene paused in her pacing. "Sporty was pretty stupid sometimes. I can say that because I loved him. I asked him how Juan reacted, and he said Juan didn't say anything, which we all know is not the best response to get from a bloodthirsty sonofabitch like

Juan Chiato. I tell you, Sporty was scared. He had a right to be scared." Darlene nodded, her eyes burning. "That all happened four weeks ago, and now look what's happened. Sporty's dead. Juan killed him, there's no doubt about it. We have to kill the bastard."

The room was silent for a full minute. Jean didn't know what to say. It did sound like Juan was probably the culprit, but who in his right mind would take revenge against someone who had a whole gang at his back? The Red Blades would reearn their name hunting down and slaughtering whoever touched Juan. And if they just happened to murder a few who were only guilty by indirect association, then so much the better. Jean regretted having asked if Carol could stay for the meeting. Sitting on the floor against the wall, Carol looked full of regrets. Darlene must have been loaded to be talking about such things so openly. Yet she appeared in full command of her senses. It was Lenny who spoke first, and Jean was surprised when he didn't dismiss Darlene's proposal outright.

"I can't understand why Sporty didn't tell me he was having trouble with Juan," he said. "He should have come to me right away, before he tried to sell any jeans. I would have told him to stay as far away as he could from the guy."

"He wanted to make his own mark," Darlene said. "He wanted to make his own money. Sporty got tired of living in your shadow and wanted to do something about it."

Lenny shifted uncomfortably. "He picked a bad way to go about it."

"We've already established that he wasn't the most intelligent guy on the planet," Carol said.

"Shut up," Darlene said. "I can say those things, but you can't. You didn't love him."

Carol made a face. "I hardly knew him."

"Let's say, for the sake of argument, that it was Juan," Lenny said. "If we want him dead, we have to do it ourselves. Anyone else will talk to someone else. And if we do kill him, it's got to look like someone else did it. Because the second Juan's Blade buddies find his body, they're going to guess it was either Darlene or me who was behind it because we were Sporty's best friends."

"I hope you're not suggesting that it has to look like an accident," Carol said.

Lenny shook his head impatiently. "If Juan has a dozen bullets in him, it can't look like an accident."

"We could run him over," Darlene suggested.

"It might be better to blow him up," Lenny said. "The less left, the better."

Jean felt compelled to speak. "Wait a second. What are we talking about here? Sporty's dead and that's terrible. But we can't avenge his death, *especially* if it was Juan who killed him. His gang will know who did it no matter how you plan it. They'll kill us all."

"Why would they kill you?" Lenny asked, an odd note in his voice.

"Because I was Sporty's friend, too," Jean said, annoyed at the question. "Because I'm here with you guys talking about this foolish plan. You can't go up against someone that's high up in a gang. It's just not done. You know that, Lenny. Why are you even listening to Darlene?"

Lenny held her eye before answering, his face dark. He hadn't appreciated her remarks. "Because I was his friend. A real friend doesn't do nothing after his friend's gunned down. I was there. He died in my arms."

Jean returned his stare. When angered, few people intimidated her. "What were you two doing at the projects so late at night?" she asked. "So close to Juan's home ground?"

Lenny didn't blink. "I didn't know about Sporty's problems with Juan. I said that already."

"But that doesn't answer my question," Jean said. "At night that piece of turf is a death zone."

"No one's asking you to be involved, Jean," Darlene said bitterly. "I just thought since Sporty always told me what a great girl you were that you'd want to be in on the payback."

"What payback is that going to be?" Jean asked, her voice hot. "Kill Juan and live in fear every second until they come for us? And who's to say they'll simply shoot us? They might torture us first. You heard about what happened to that teenage bookie that the police found on Main? During the autopsy they found a pillowcase in his stomach. Do you know how scared someone has to be to swallow a pillowcase? Oh, and did I forget to mention that his throat had been cut from ear to ear? That was down on Main, Darlene— Red Blade territory, Juan's playing ground."

"Was it a *whole* pillow case?" Carol asked.

"Oh, would you shut up," Jean said this time.

Darlene glared at Jean. "I thought you were more than a chicken bitch. I guess I was wrong."

Jean turned to Lenny, her boyfriend, the father of her unborn child. He still hadn't answered her original question. Earlier she had been right to think of him as a stranger. Looking at his dark, cold masklike face, she hardly recognized him. And to think, she had made love to him only two days before on this very couch. No, she had had sex with him—there was a difference.

"How can you let her talk to me that way?" she asked. "This is your house. Kick her out. You know she's talking crap. You know this whole meeting is insane."

Lenny took his time answering. Something on the floor between his legs had him fascinated. It must have been the dirt because that was all that was there. The heavy burdens on his attention—the filth and her request. Finally he spoke, his head still down.

"You just didn't care about him the way we did. You can't understand." He shrugged, adding, "We can't let Juan get away with it."

Jean jumped up from the sofa, feeling the blood suffuse her face. "I cared about him more than any of you know! I knew him before any of you knew him! But he's dead, and it's really sad, but why do we have to die with him? Why do we even have to talk about killing people?" Her throat choked with emotion; her voice came out cracked. "Why do we even have to live like this?"

Jean didn't wait for an answer to her painful questions. She ran from the living room, into the bedroom, and out onto Lenny's balcony. The platform was a haphazard affair, a collection of splintered planks thrown on top of a randomly spaced group of termite-zapped wooden stilts. Yet the drop to the ground was substantial: thirty feet straight down. Jean heard the boards of the railing creak as she leaned against them. The view was pretty at least, if you liked smelly oil wells and rundown houses that doubled as fear-infested fortresses. The downtown skyscrapers were visible, far in the distance; dark towers with dots of light in a bleary haze of pollutants. Really, Jean thought, it was all the same no matter which direction she turned. It wasn't a city, it was a dying monster. She wanted it to die. She wanted the big bombs to fall, the red mushroom clouds to form. She didn't know why she had argued so passionately for life when she felt so little life in her heart. It was ironic that ever since the seed of a new human being had started growing in her body she had felt more and more like ending it all. Not suicide, no, but something close to it. Something like a contract that could be entered into without serious penalties. Not a devil's contract certainly, more like a person-to-person handshake and a pat on the back and an understanding that it was OK. That it would be all right.

I did the best I could, God, but it wasn't good enough. But I don't hate you and I don't hate myself. I just don't know what the hell I'm doing. Help, please, help me.

Standing on the creaky balcony, time passed for Jean Rodrigues.

How much time, she didn't know.

But somewhere in the sand at the bottom of Jean Rodrigues's fallen hourglass, the colors of the night-time city altered. The dull yellows turned to blues and the sober reds to fresh greens. The intensity of the light grew as well, as one after another tiny candles were lit in dark corners above homes that had never been built and atop skyscrapers that would never fall.

The shift was subtle at first, and she didn't know it was even happening to her until she suddenly found herself staring out upon a landscape bathed in pulsing light. It was only then that she realized she was back in her dream, being given the chance again to lift up her arms and fly, over the wall and into the land where the wishes and the wisher were one. It was a chance she was not going to pass up twice. There, she thought eagerly, there, make me immortal.

Happy at last, still leaning against the railing, she lifted her arms.

But Jean did not fly; the human body could not. The floor of the balcony abruptly vanished from beneath her feet and she fell instead. Headfirst toward a ground that took forever to reach. Yet the plunge was not terrifying, as Shari Cooper's fall from a balcony one year earlier had been. The contract was signed and sealed. It wasn't suicide but an accident. Or at the very least someone else's fault. There would be no penalty for Jean Rodrigues. There would be no more pain.

CHAPTER

III

*F*LOATING DOWNSTREAM in a boat on a river, you can see only a little way in front of you, a little way behind, the nearby shore, and if you're lucky and the river isn't lined with trees, maybe a far-off field or house. But if you go up in a plane and look down at the river, you can see the entire course of the waterway. You can see where it began, and you know where it will end. In a sense, the aerial view is like being given a vision of the future, at least as far as the life of the river is concerned.

Death is a vision that never dies. I am supposed to be dead, but I experience the entirety of my life as if it were all happening at once. I float above the river of personality that was once Shari Ann Cooper. I know her, I am her, but I am something else now as well, something blissful. Even as I poke into the dark corners of my life, my joy does not leave me. It is separate from personalities and events. My joy is what I am and has no name.

I did many things in my eighteen years on planet

Earth. I was born. I learned to walk, to talk, to laugh, and to sing. I learned to cry as well, and I chased boys. I even got laid once. I was popular. My junior year, mine was voted the best smile in the whole high school. But few of the things that I considered important on Earth interest me now. As I view the whole of my life, a seemingly insignificant event holds my attention. I was sixteen years old. There was a girl in my biology class who was deaf, not a crime in itself, but she was homely as well. Those were two big strikes against her with my friends, and two strikes were completely unforgivable in those days. No one ever talked to her—I didn't either—or even thought about her, except occasionally to wonder why she wasn't in a special school. It never occurred to me that she might be a brave soul trying to live a normal life despite her handicap.

There was one day, though, as I was leaving biology class after the bell had rung, that I noticed the girl was having trouble finding her glasses. On top of everything else she couldn't see well and I knew that she would sometimes remove her glasses while the teacher talked and just sit with her eyes closed, trying, so it seemed to me, to absorb the lesson by osmosis. I didn't know at the time that someone had swiped her glasses, but I did know she was going to have a hard time making it to her next class without them. I walked over and gently tapped her on the shoulder. I scared her, made her jump, and immediately felt bad about it. But she smiled quickly at me after she'd recovered and squinted. I wasn't sure how much of me she could see.

"Hi," I said. "Can I help you?"

She leaned forward, closer to my mouth, and gestured for me to repeat myself. I realized she was reading my lips. I put my face right in front of hers and asked my question again. This time she nodded vigorously. She gestured that she couldn't find her glasses and if I would help her look for them. I didn't have to look long to realize someone must have taken them. I mean, it wasn't like there were a lot of hiding places on a school desk. I placed my face in front of hers again.

"Lost," I said. "Gone. Stolen. I will help you."

The news seemed to take her aback, but only for a moment. She nodded, collected her books, and stood up. She offered me her arm; clearly I would have to touch her to help lead her to her next class. I didn't mind, although at that time—that week I think it was—it was something of a taboo to touch anyone of the same sex. In fact, I was happy to help her. Very happy I had finally stopped to speak to her.

Her name was Candice, but she said to call her Candy in her uninflected, flat speech. I helped her around for the next two days while she waited for new glasses to arrive. We never did find out what happened to the original pair. During that time I learned to sign quite a few words. We became friends, and I learned something else as well—that life was good even when it was hard. That hidden beauty was much greater than physical beauty. Candy could not hear our teachers, she could hardly see them. But she taught me more than any of them had. I was sad the day I heard she would be coming to school no more. She had ended up returning to a special school for deaf kids, after all. I missed her.

But what I didn't know at the time was that from the moment the thought occurred to me to help Candy, and all the time I was with her, tidal waves of light and energy rolled from me and spread out over the entire universe, to the farthest planet circling the loneliest star in the most distant galaxy. I touched that much. But I could only see these waves as I reviewed my life when my life was over. My good grades, my good looks—none of that had mattered. None of it had affected the creation, but my simple act of service and kindness had been like a miracle. And the strange thing was that I had helped Candy only because I wanted to. Because, for once, I had stopped thinking of myself and thought only of someone else. As I watched the beginning and the middle and the end of the river of Shari Cooper, I could see then the answer to one of our age-old riddles. Does love survive? Yes, I thought, somewhere in some place it is saved and made sacred. I had not known how much love Candy had given to me, and how much I had given to her.

I had known nothing.

"Good," a voice said.

I opened my eyes and found myself sitting on a grassy bank on a sunny day beside a gently flowing stream. The still air was warm, fragrant, radiant with light and good feelings. In the distance were trees, snow-capped mountains, but no houses, no roads. I was in paradise but I wasn't alone. Beside me sat an extraordinary man.

He appeared to be thirty years old. He had an austere face, hollow cheeks, deepset blue eyes, a soft smile. It was difficult to specify his race. His skin was a deep coppery color; he could have been an ancient Egyptian priest come to life before me. Perhaps he was, I thought. He wore a blue silk robe. I had on the same clothes I had died in: green pants and a yellow blouse. I was going to have to change one of these days, I thought. My surroundings were pervaded by peace, but the man's aura was even more tranquil. I had no memory of seeing him before, yet I felt as if I had known him a long time. His smile widened at my thought.

"Very good, Shari," he said. Like his smile, his voice was soft, yet it carried great authority behind it. He was not someone with whom I would have argued.

I smiled. "Can you read my mind?"

"Yes. Do you want me to stop?"

"It doesn't matter. You were with me as I reviewed my life. I felt you."

"Yes. How do you feel about how you did?"

"Like a fool."

"That's a good way to feel. Only a fool can get into heaven."

"Is that where we are? Did I make it?"

"I joke with you. All this you see is just a thought. You created this place because you still feel the need to occupy a certain space and time. People usually carry that habit with them when they cross over. It is to be expected; it is fine. But you don't need to talk to me with a body. When you feel comfortable, you may drop it."

I rubbed my legs with my open palms. They felt the same as they had on Earth. "I'm still sort of used to this body." I paused, troubled. "But I suppose it's really back on Earth rotting in a grave somewhere."

"Is that real, Shari? After all you have experienced, would you say that any part of you could rot?"

I frowned. "I'm not sure I understand. I do know I have a soul and that it survived death. I learned that the hard way. But my body died. It's still on Earth. I saw them bury it. I went to my own funeral."

"I was there."

"Really? You should have introduced yourself. What is your name? Do you have one?"

"You may call me by a name." He considered. "Call me the Rishi. Rishi means 'seer.' When I was in a physical body, people often called me that."

"So you've been on Earth?"

"Yes. We're on Earth now, Shari."

I was amazed. I looked around. "Are we in Switzerland?"

He laughed softly. "We are in another dimension of Earth. But these concepts—distance, space, time—they have no meaning for you now, unless you give them meaning. You're free of those limitations. You can be on any world in the universe just by wishing it."

His words made me smile. "How is Peter? Where is he?"

"Not far. You'll see him soon."

"Good. I mean, don't get me wrong, I like being here with you, but I want to know why you're here with me. What our relationship is." I stopped. "Am I asking too many questions?"

"I'm here to take your questions. When people first cross over, they often go through a question-and-answer period like this. But understand that not all your questions can be answered with words. Our relationship is a beautiful thing. We are, ultimately, the same person, the same being. But if that is too abstract a concept for you, then think of a huge oversoul made up of many souls. Throughout many lives on many worlds, these different souls learn and grow. Each life is like a day in class, and as you know, some people do better in class than others, but all will graduate if they keep going." He paused. "We are a part of the same oversoul, Shari."

"But you've already graduated?" I asked.

"Yes."

"To where? To what?"

He gestured around him. "To all that is. To God if you like. I see your surprise, but it is so. Yes, I am with God now as I speak to you. I see you as my Goddess." He reached over and touched my hand, his fingers warm, soothing. "You are very dear to me, Shari."

I felt so loved then I began to cry. He was like my big brother Jimmy. Or my father even, my real father, whom I had never known. I realized then that even when I had been alive he had been with me, just out of sight, helping me, guiding me. It meant so much to me to be able to see him again with my eyes. I felt as if finally I had come home. I clasped his hand in mine.

"Will you stay with me?" I asked.

"Yes. Always I am with you."

I laughed, I felt so foolish for weeping. "Wow. Who would have thought it would be like this?"

"That you would die and end up in Switzerland with an ancient Egyptian priest?" he asked with a twinkle in his eye. "I was in Egypt a long time ago as people *on* Earth measure time. I am there now. I teach beside the pyramids. People call me Master."

I was fascinated that he could be in many places at the same time, even as he lived outside of time. "What do you teach?" I asked.

"Hmm. Big question. I will give a short answer." He considered for a moment. "The teachings of a Master appear different in different times. The needs of the time and the place vary. When you were alive few would have said the words of Buddha matched those of Krishna or Jesus. But in essence they all said the same thing—that there is one God and that we are all part of him. That it is important to realize this great truth while we are on Earth. But over time the message becomes distorted. People take God out of man and put him up in an imaginary heaven, where he is of no use to anyone. Or else they found a religion based on the worship of a particular Master. Yet Buddha never founded Buddhism. Christ never founded Christianity. Krishna hardly spoke about religion at all. He was too busy dancing and playing his flute. He was too ecstatic to be dogmatic. I am very happy now as I speak to my followers in ancient Egypt. But I know a short time after I vanish from their view they will begin to squabble over what I really said and what I really meant. Even now they quarrel amongst themselves. I have to laugh—it is natural that a Master should speak from his level of consciousness but that his followers should hear the words at their level. A long time ago, as mortals are fond of saying, the Rishi was also worshiped as the only son of God. But we all deserve that title, don't you think?"

I nodded. "How about saying 'the daughter of God'?"

Christopher Pike

"Very good. You understand, I am not saying religion is bad. Where it turns men and women inward and helps them realize that they are as great as the creator who created them, that there is an ocean of love and silence deep within the heart, then it is useful. But where it divides people against one another, where one person is led to believe he is saved and another is damned, or where it leads a person to think that true happiness will be found only in an afterlife, then it is harmful. Each life on Earth is very precious. I called each one a day in class, but if you are wise, if you go deep inside, you can go all the way to the goal in just one life." He paused. "It's a wonderful thing to be alive."

I sat up with a start. "That's a line from the story that I wrote before I left."

"I know."

"Did you help me write that story?"

"Yes. And it has not been lost. Your brother saved it. He read it and believes it to be true. It means much to him. He keeps it safe."

There were tears in my eyes again. "That was my last wish before I left. To be remembered. How is Jimmy?"

"He's fine. He thinks about you often."

I dabbed at my eyes. "What I wouldn't give to see him again, to tell him I'm all right." I stopped and shook my head. "Here I am in paradise with you and I'm still complaining. I guess I'll never learn. I can't see him until he dies and I don't want him to die until he's an old man. I guess I'll have to wait."

The Rishi took his hand back. He stared at me with his beautiful eyes—the color of limitless sky. I sensed the joy behind them, but also the power of eternity. I knew I was safe in his company, yet something in his expression made me shiver. He was as gentle as an angel, but I sensed he could also be as firm as a king. I was still in class, I realized. He was the teacher. It was wise to listen to him.

"You don't have to wait," he said.

"What do you mean? I thought you said Jimmy was fine?"

"He is. But you can go back."

"To Earth? To a physical body? So soon? Will I be born as a baby?"

"No. You can, if you want, become what we call a Wanderer. You can enter the body of an eighteen-year-old girl."

I had never heard of such an idea. "Is that legal? I mean, what will happen to the girl? Won't she go running to the nearest priest for an exorcist to get me out of her?"

"She will leave the body altogether. She'll be fine. She's already made this choice. At night, when she sleeps, her soul converses with me. She feels she is going nowhere in her life. She wants to give you another chance. Her leaving is purely her choice. It is always that way." He paused. "She'll be with me."

"Who is this girl?" I asked.

"Her name is Jean Rodrigues. If you wish, that will soon be your name."

CHAPTER

IV

*T*HE FIRST SENSATION Jean Rodrigues felt was of pressure, as if she were under a thousand feet of water. Every square inch of her skin was being smothered. She wanted to cry out, to shove the water away, but was unable to make a sound or move. For a while she struggled in a black place, then she felt a prick of something cold and sharp, and her struggling ceased, at least for a little while.

Time went by, jumbled moments of consciousness and unconsciousness. Next, she heard voices. They seemed to come from far off, and she listened to them for what could have been hours before realizing that they belonged to her mother and Carol. She could make no sense of the words except to realize that they both sounded worried. She was about to doze off again, when someone shook her roughly. She moved to push the person away; she really didn't want to wake up yet. But she couldn't find her hand so she opened her eyes instead. Her mother was standing

40

over her with bloodshot eyes. It looked as if her mother hadn't slept in a long time. Jean wondered where the hell she was.

"*Mamá,*" she said softly.

Her mother glanced at someone to the side. "*Gracias a Dios,* she's awake," she said.

That someone came into view. It was Carol. She also looked exhausted. "How do you feel, Jean?" Carol asked, concerned.

"Tired." She coughed weakly. "Thirsty. Where am I?"

Her mother thrust her hand out and then held a glass of water to Jean's lips. "Sip this. You'll feel better."

Jean did as she was told. She realized her lips were badly parched, bleeding even. The water went down cool and delicious. Her heart pounded at the back of her skull. Her head did not hurt so much as it felt as if it were being steadily squeezed by a clamp. She swallowed and gestured for her mother to take away the glass. Her vision went beyond them, to the hallway beyond the open door. She saw nurses walking back and forth. She was in a hospital, she thought.

"What happened?" she asked.

Her mother and Carol looked at each other as if deciding how much to tell her. "There was an accident," her mother finally said.

"Lenny's bedroom balcony collapsed," Carol added.

"You fell down the hill and hit your head and broke a few ribs," her mother continued. "But now that you're awake, you're going to be all right. But I have to say you gave us quite a scare for a couple of days there."

"A couple of days?" Jean whispered. "What day is it?"

"It's Monday morning," her mother said. "You've been unconscious this whole time." Her eyes dampened as she leaned over and hugged her daughter gently. Jean had to stifle a groan. Her right side was extraordinarily sensitive. She wondered if the *few* broken ribs really meant her whole side was caved in. Clearly, to be unconscious as long as she had been, she must have suffered a serious concussion. Her mother added, "My poor girl."

Jean patted her mother's head. "Don't worry, *Mamá,* I feel better than I probably look. I'll be out of here in no time. How're my brothers and sisters doing?"

Her mother sat up and smiled. "Why, that's sweet of you to ask, since you're the one who needs special attention right now. They're fine. I'll call them and tell them you're awake." She stood. "In fact, I'll go tell the doctor. I think he'll want to examine you."

Jean smiled. "Is he cute? Did he examine me while I was asleep?"

Carol and her mother chuckled; they seemed so relieved. "He couldn't keep his hands off you," Carol said.

Her mother stepped toward the door. "I'll be back in a few minutes. Try sipping a little more water, Jean. Carol, maybe you can help her."

"Cierto, Mrs. Rodrigues," Carol said.

"Mamá," Jean said. "Has Lenny been by to see me?"

Her mother hesitated at the door. Again she and Carol exchanged looks. "Yes," her mother said. "He's been by."

"Could you call him as well?" Jean said. "Tell him I'd like some flowers and chocolates and an immediate visit."

Her mother lowered her head and nodded. "I will." She went to leave.

"Mamá," Jean said.

Her mother paused once more. "Yes?"

"Te amo," Jean said.

Her mother had to take a breath. The words had caught her by surprise. Again her eyes dampened— no, this time they spilled over and tears ran down her cheeks. "My," she said, touching her heart. "I haven't heard that in a long time. I love you, too, Jean. I'll be back as soon as I can."

When she was gone, Jean gestured for Carol to help her sit up. Carol picked a remote control off the nightstand. "This will make the top half of the bed move up," Carol said. "That way you won't have to bend so much. Ready?"

"Yes," Jean said. Carol pushed the button and the top of the bed moved her into a sitting position. The shift in the blood supply in her body brought a wave of new aches and pains. It felt as if her right knee was pretty screwed up as well; there was, in fact, a thick bandage wrapped around her right leg from the top of her calf to halfway up her thigh. An IV ran into the back of her left hand. But she didn't feel any bandages on her ribs beneath her wrinkled green hospital gown. She wondered what had become of her clothes. Carol carefully sat on the bed beside her. Jean offered her her right hand and Carol took it.

"You really had us scared," Carol said.

"Have you been here a lot?" Jean asked.

"Most of the time. To tell you the truth, the doctor didn't know if you were going to wake up or not. Not until early this morning."

"He could tell then?"

"*Sí.* Don't ask me how. It was only this morning they moved you out of intensive care. You should have seen yourself yesterday and the day before. You had a ton of tubes and wires hooked up to your body."

"Sounds kinky." Jean considered. "What's the deal with Lenny?"

"What are you talking about?"

"What you and my mother are afraid to talk about. I saw the looks you gave each other when I asked about him. What's going on? Why isn't he here?"

Carol sighed; she was trapped. "Jean, what do you remember about last Friday night?"

Jean frowned. "Everything, I think, up until I fell. I remember we had that stupid fight about whether to waste Juan or not. Then I ran out onto the balcony. I remember staring out over the city." She paused. "And the fireworks."

"What fireworks?"

"There weren't any fireworks?"

Carol laughed. "You must have seen those after you fell."

"No. I remember—just before I fell—the whole city was lit up with colored lights. And I felt so happy." She stopped and shook her head. "But you're right, they couldn't have been fireworks. Who would be setting them off in the middle of the night?" She studied Carol. Her friend had yet to answer her question. "You tell me what happened last Friday. Where were you when I fell?"

"I was in my car, on my way home."

"What? You left Lenny's house without me?"

Carol shrugged. "Lenny told me to go. Jean, don't look at me that way. You were out on that balcony for so long. It didn't look like you were ever coming back in."

"How long is *so long?*"

"More than half an hour."

"I wasn't out there that long. No way."

"Yes, you were. I came up behind you and called your name and you ignored me. You were out there at least thirty minutes when I left the house."

"Was Darlene still there when you left?"

"Yes." Carol thought for a moment. "It might have been Darlene who said I should go, instead of Lenny. Yeah, I think it was her."

"And you just did what she said without talking to me first?"

"I told you, I tried to get your attention but you weren't answering. I figured you wanted to be alone. Or at least alone with Lenny."

"This is too weird. What does Lenny say happened?"

Carol hesitated. "I don't know. I haven't talked to him."

"Why not?"

Carol averted her eyes. "I don't know how to tell

45

you this. Lenny was on the balcony when you fell. He fell with you. He's in this hospital right now, but he's in worse shape than you."

Jean could feel her heart pound. "How worse?"

Carol's eyes filled. "He broke his back in the fall. It looks like he's paralyzed from the waist down."

"Oh, God," Jean whispered. She thought of Lenny's beautiful body, his powerful legs—now as good as dead. How could this have happened? Why did the balcony suddenly collapse? Carol was shaking her head.

"I'm sorry," she said. "I wasn't trying to keep the truth from you. It's just that your mother didn't think we should tell you when you woke up. She wanted to wait until you were stronger."

"I understand," Jean said softly, staring at the far wall, seeing only wheelchairs and impassable stairways, boredom and despair for Lenny. He was so active—how would he be able to live? She added, "Is there anything else you want to tell me? That you were afraid to tell me?"

Carol raised her head and nodded. "There is one other thing. The fall was rough on you. While you were unconscious, you began to bleed, you know, down there. You lost the *bebé,* Jean."

Jean blinked. "What baby?"

"Your baby. You were pregnant, remember?"

Jean couldn't keep up with the barrage of information. It was true she could remember buying and taking the E.P.T., and failing it. She could also remember telling Carol about it. Yet, at the same time, she had trouble accepting the fact that she had indeed been pregnant. Like it was something that could not possibly have happened to her, not under ordinary circumstances. But there was no arguing with the facts. Strangely, she felt neither relief nor a sense of loss that the baby was gone. She simply felt nothing, as if the whole matter had been someone else's problem.

"Does my mother know I was pregnant?" Jean asked.

"Yes. The doctor told her, after your miscarriage. She took it well. She didn't freak out or anything."

"*Bueno.* Anything else?"

Carol smiled sadly. "No. Except that I'm glad you're awake and feeling better."

Jean patted Carol's hand. "You're a good friend. Thank you for staying with me while I was out. I won't forget that."

Carol did a double take. "I've never heard you talk that way before."

"Talk what way?"

"I don't know, just the way you're talking. You sound nicer than usual."

Jean nodded. "Maybe the fall did me some good."

Her mother returned with Dr. Snapple, who must have changed his name to his favorite drink because there was no disguising the fact that he had been born in the Middle East. Dr. Snapple had a thick accent and a face so dark he could have been conceived staring into the sun. He was a big man with fingers as thick as Cuban cigars. Jean didn't find him attractive but competent, preferable for a physician. Dr. Snapple asked her a few questions about how she felt and did a number of tests involving her vision. The results seemed to satisfy him, but when he touched her right side and the back of her head she groaned. Not mentioning her miscarriage, he explained that her concussion and broken ribs would take time to heal, that there was no magic procedure to speed her recovery. At the same time, he said she was to stay in the hospital for at least two more days, possibly three or four. Jean fretted over the cost. She had no insurance.

"Why can't I go home now?" she asked. "If you can't do anything for me?"

"Because you have been unconscious for over two days," he said. "Who's to say you might not slip back into a coma? We have to keep you for observation."

"But I won't go back into a coma," Jean said. "It's not possible."

Dr. Snapple was amused. "Since when did you develop the ability to see inside your own brain?"

Jean was annoyed. She knew her mother was too proud to accept help from the state. "I don't need to see inside my head to know how I feel. *Mamá*, I shouldn't stay here, you know. How are we going to pay for it?"

Her mother was staring at her. "You're worried about that? You're not worried about yourself?"

"Of course I'm worried about the money," Jean said. "We don't have any."

Her mother smiled faintly. "Don't worry, Jean, we'll find a way." She glanced at Dr. Snapple. "Thank you, Doctor. I'll make sure she stays here, and in bed."

Dr. Snapple left and a few minutes later Carol

excused herself. For a moment Jean was alone with her mother. It was obvious to Jean that her mother had suffered terribly while she had been unconscious, and that the poor woman didn't know what to say or do now that the worst was over. Jean didn't know if anything had to be said. She just held her mother's hand and smiled at her, and after a while her mother seemed to feel better. Her mother kissed her goodbye and promised to come that evening, after work. She also warned Jean about staying in bed.

The moment she was gone, Jean got up. She lasted all of five seconds before a wave of dizziness made her sit down quickly. All right, she thought, her brain had to get used to gravity again. Taking several deep breaths, she got up slowly, then sat back down before she could fall over. She did this a few times and eventually was able to stand without feeling as if she were strapped to a Ferris wheel. Her side hurt awfully, as did her right knee. She wondered what she had looked like when they found her. She hadn't heard Lenny come up behind her on the balcony. Not that she could remember, anyway.

Jean knew she wouldn't rest until she saw him.

She limped across the room and found her clothes in the closet. The hospital dry cleaning service hadn't been by since Friday. She saw instantly how much she had bled. Her jeans and top were both stained dark red. She didn't know what to do. The green hospital gown she wore was drafty; she didn't want to go strolling down the halls with her ass hanging out, although she thought she had a very nice ass. Indeed, glancing over her shoulder at her bare behind, she was pleased to see she was still curvaceous even after her special coma diet.

Jean searched the closet for a robe but didn't find one. She was about to give up and return to bed when she noticed a door in the corner opposite the closet, one that didn't appear to lead into the hallway. Cracking it open a couple of inches she discovered— big surprise—that it led into an adjoining room. Her neighbor was a seventy-year-old white woman with a snore like Fred Flintstone's and a wardrobe the equal of Elizabeth Taylor's. The woman had so many clothes jammed in her closet it was as if she planned to attend numerous costume balls on the other side in case she failed to check out of the hospital. Jean took one glance at the woman stretched out on the bed and figured the woman would never know if she was missing a dress or not.

And so, not many minutes later, wearing a long print gown that she wouldn't have been caught dead in under other circumstances, Jean went searching for Lenny. She sneaked out of her wing without difficulty, but by the time she reached the hospital lobby she had to sit down to rest. She couldn't decide which hurt worse, her head, her leg, or her side. All together, though, it was one nasty ache. Yet the strange thing was that the pain bothered her only as far as her body was concerned. It didn't depress her *inside* that she was injured. She accepted it so well she actually surprised herself.

When she was sufficiently recovered, Jean strolled up to a woman at the reception area. She did her best to appear of sound body and mind but the huge bandage around her head was not something she could make vanish with witty conversation. To make matters worse, the bandage was even stained with blood. But the elderly woman behind the counter didn't seem to notice. She looked up as Jean approached.

"Can I help you, miss?" she asked.

"Yes," Jean said. "My brother, Lenny Mandez, is staying in this hospital. He broke his back last Friday. Could you please tell me his floor and room number?"

The woman put a hand to her mouth. "The poor dear. Is he going to be all right?"

Jean had to swallow before answering. She wondered what it would be like to see him. She reminded herself that she mustn't break down. "I hope so."

The woman turned to her computer. "How do you spell that last name?"

Jean gave her the name letter by letter. She thought it wiser to act like Lenny's sister rather than his girlfriend because surely he was still in intensive care and there might be restrictions as far as visitors were concerned. Indeed, a moment later the woman confirmed her suspicion that he was not in a normal room.

"He's on the eighth floor, Room Nine," the woman said. "That's a restricted area. You might have to show I.D. to get in."

"No problem," Jean said. "Thanks for your help."

"You look like you've been in an accident yourself," the woman observed.

"Yeah, I fell off a balcony."

"You were lucky you weren't killed."

Jean felt a cold wave, goose bumps all over. Had someone just walked over her grave? Felt like it. "Yeah," she muttered.

Room Nine turned out to be many small adjoining cubicles hooked up by wires and computers to a central nurses' station. One thing they didn't worry about in intensive care was people's privacy, Jean thought. The area was thick with the smell of alcohol and pain. The moment Jean walked in, she had to sit down. Her head throbbed. A young nurse who looked like a nun came over to check on her. Jean assured the nurse she was fine and explained how she was there to see her brother. The woman recognized Lenny's name. She didn't ask for I.D. Jean was helped into the last cubicle on the left and left alone with her boyfriend.

He was not a pretty sight, and it broke her heart because he had been such a pretty boy. Surprisingly, he was not in a body cast but held rigidly in place by a combination of plastic rods and screws and clamps. His bed, it was clear, was capable of rotating so that his body could be turned. Jean suspected it was necessary to circulate his blood and keep him from getting bed sores. He had no marks on his face, no wounds to any part of the front of his body, although she could see the edge of the large bandage on his back. Still, he looked like death itself. His skin was pasty white, as if a vampire on a binge got hold of him. His eyes were closed; he appeared to be asleep.

"Lenny," she whispered, her voice shaky.

He opened his eyes, but didn't look over at her, staring at the ceiling instead. "Jean," he said softly.

She moved to his side, went to take his hand, then

thought better of it. The simple fear of touching him hurt her as much as anything had so far. It must have hurt him as well; he looked at her with such wounded eyes it was all she could do to not burst out crying. She remembered a dog she had had as a child. He had looked at her the same way right after being struck by a car, right before he died.

"'Ola," she said.

"'Ola," he said. "How are you?"

"Fine." She touched her bandage. "Just bumped my head is all."

"Yesterday they told me you were in a coma."

"That was yesterday." She paused. "How's your back?"

He smiled bitterly. "I don't know. I can't feel it."

"What can you feel?"

He closed his eyes. "I can use my hands and arms. I don't know what else works."

She reached over and gently touched his big toe. He had on underwear, nothing else, but there was a vaporizer steaming in the corner and the cubicle was warm and humid.

"Can you feel that?" she asked.

"Feel what?" His eyes remained closed.

She took her hand away, the weight on her chest heavier than the one on her head. "Nothing. Lenny. Look at me, please, I need to talk to you."

He opened his eyes. "What do you want to talk about?"

She fretted with her hands and had to make herself stop. "You're going to get better."

His voice was flat. "No, I'm not. The doctor says my spinal cord's been severed. It won't heal, they never do. I'm crippled for life. I'm screwed, that's a simple fact. So don't stand there with that little bump on your head and tell me I'm going to get better."

Her throat choked with grief. "I'm sorry."

He turned his head the other way. "I don't want your sympathy."

"What do you want?"

"To be left alone. Get out of here and don't come back."

Finally her tears came; she couldn't stop them. "You don't mean that."

He turned his head back in her direction. His eyes were red, with anger as well as pain. "But I do, Jean. I can't stand to see you walking around while I'm stuck here in this bed."

"Damn you!" she yelled. "That's not fair! Just because I'm not paralyzed I can't be your girlfriend anymore?"

"My *girlfriend?*" he said sarcastically. "How can I have a girlfriend? I can't even control when I have to go to the bathroom anymore, never mind have sex. I'm no good to you. I'm no good to anybody."

"I don't care what you can and can't do. All that matters is that you're alive." She dared to touch his hand. "I mean it, I'm not going to leave you. We can work on you getting better together. And if you're unable to make a full recovery, then we'll work on that as well."

He looked down where she touched him. His eyes seemed to soften. "I can feel that," he whispered.

She nodded eagerly. *"Bueno."*

Unfortunately, the softness only went so deep. He

shut his eyes and turned away again. "I have to sleep, Jean. I'm very tired."

She leaned over and kissed his hand. "I'll be back," she said.

He did not respond. He needed time, she told herself as she left the cubicle. Time and love. She couldn't remember having ever loved him so much.

CHAPTER
V

*T*HE RISHI WALKED WITH ME beside the stream. I still found it hard to understand how I had created the paradise we were enjoying when I had never imagined a scene so beautiful. The flowers that bloomed beside the water were like none found on Earth—or at least the Earth I knew—so many different colors and shapes. The joy of existence, of walking with this great being, was like a constant stream of gladness inside my chest, as clear and sweet as the water at our feet. I questioned him about Wanderers.

"Were there any on Earth that I knew personally?" I asked.

"You met many as Shari Cooper. But you weren't close to any."

"How about in history? Were any famous people Wanderers?"

"That is a perceptive question. The answer is yes, many well-known people were Wanderers. To be a Wanderer is a great honor as well as a great sacrifice. A soul has to be highly evolved in order to bypass the birth process. Because a Wanderer enters into a developed physical body, he—or she, sex is, of course, not an issue here—carries more of the knowledge of the spiritual plane with him to Earth. Always, he returns to the physical plane with a particular mission, and because he radiates so much soul energy, he often succeeds. By nature, Wanderers are charismatic, intelligent, loving. People are attracted to them. They want to be with them."

"Have you ever been a Wanderer?"

The Rishi smiled. "I wander all over the place."

"Will you ever return to Earth again?"

"I am on Earth now."

"I mean, somewhere in the time frame that I understand to be modern society?"

"Perhaps. It is up to God."

"Does he talk to you? I mean, like I am talking to you now?"

"God is an unbounded ocean of light and consciousness. I float in that ocean on whatever current or wave arises. I go with that, it is my joy to do so. I talk to God when I talk to you. I see God when I see the trees. I feel God when I touch my head. Who is there to talk to but myself?" The Rishi chuckled. "I'm sorry, I don't know how to answer your question."

I smiled. "It doesn't matter. Your answer was beautiful. Tell me some of the famous people on Earth who were Wanderers?"

"They're often hard to spot, but they do have one quality that makes them stand out from others. At one point in their lives they all undergo a huge change of heart and awareness. That, of course, is when the new soul enters the body. Einstein was an example. From a young age he was intelligent, but not the genius he became when the Wanderer who brought the theory of relativity to Earth arrived. That was his mission, to bring that knowledge."

"But wasn't the atomic bomb developed as a result of his theories?"

"Yes. His knowledge was insightful. But it is up to mankind to decide what to do with such knowledge. The theories themselves were neither good nor bad."

"Who was another example of a Wanderer?"

"Martin Luther King. I think his purpose must be obvious to you. But this will surprise you—Malcom X was also a Wanderer."

"Him? But wasn't he a bigot?"

"He was many things while on Earth. Can any man or woman be defined by one word? But the Malcolm X whom history will remember entered while he was in jail. Immediately there was a huge change in his outlook. He became interested in religious matters. Many Wanderers go through this phase because in your society, religion is seen as the main source of spirituality, although, in reality, that is a great misunderstanding. But as I said, religion has its purpose and Malcolm X became deeply religious. He was extremely charismatic. He drew people by the thousands."

"But wasn't he a Black Muslim? Didn't he hate white people?"

"You just came from a predominantly Judeo-Christian society. Both Judaism and Christianity are fine religions, as are Islam, Buddhism, and Hinduism. One is not better than the other, no matter what the priests and ministers and rabbis would have you believe. Where religion awakens divine love, it is useful. Where it narrows the mind with dogma, it is harmful. And it is true that Malcolm X spent much of his adult life trying to separate Caucasians from African-Americans. But we must come back to what his mission as a Wanderer was. He came to give pride to people of color. At the time many African-Americans, particularly young males, felt a certain helplessness as far as dealing with society. Malcolm X showed them how to be proud and strong."

"But doesn't pride divide people?"

"It can. But it was a necessary step for that segment of population *at that time.* You cannot let go of pride until you've first had it. Malcolm X stirred things up—that was his purpose. You cannot judge people such as him. You cannot judge anybody."

"But if he was a Wanderer, why was he assassinated? Why didn't he have divine protection?"

"He had divine protection. But when a Wanderer is finished with his mission, he often leaves suddenly. Either in a blaze of bullets or quietly."

"Was Malcolm X happy when he got over here?"

"He did not accomplish everything he set out to accomplish. He was used by others, and his mission was distorted. But that happens. He had no regrets. Regret is the most useless of all emotions."

"I'm confused. You speak as if when he entered the body he didn't know he was a Wanderer?"

"That is correct. Few Wanderers realize what they are while in a physical body, at least consciously. But deep inside they know they are on Earth for a reason. They usually move toward their particular mission spontaneously."

"Will I realize that I'm a Wanderer?"

"It's possible. It's up to you. You have free will."

"What will my mission be?"

"I speak of missions because it gives you some understanding of why you would want to return. But in reality there is only one mission—to realize divine love. To awaken that divine love in others. But different people do that in different ways, and they don't have to be Wanderers to inspire others. Every man and woman born into a physical body on Earth has a mission. Your particular one will be to inspire the often forgotten segment of the poor Hispanic community. Jean Rodrigues is Hispanic and poor. As her, you will write stories that millions of people will read. They will not necessarily be spiritual stories. They can be about space ships or aliens or dragons or ordinary people. The topic does not matter. But the spirituality will be in your stories because it's inside you. It will flow into your words. People will read your stories and without understanding why, yearn for something greater. And because you are a young Hispanic woman, you will also serve as a role model for other young people like Jean Rodrigues."

I smiled. "I always wanted to be a writer. But where will I get my ideas? Will I have a muse?"

The Rishi smiled. "You will be inspired, don't worry. But perhaps you can write a story about where you get your ideas. I imagine it would be very popular."

"This is great. I couldn't ask for a better job. I loved writing that story about what happened to me when I died. Do you think I'll be able to find my brother and get my story published?"

He regarded me fondly. "It's possible."

"What does that look mean? You know something I don't. Will I find Jimmy?"

"Yes."

I clapped my hands together. "Great! Will I recognize him as my brother?"

"That is up to you."

I stopped walking. "But I have to know him. Can't you help me out here?"

The Rishi was amused. "I am always helping you, Shari."

"I know that. I appreciate that. But what can I do after I get in Jean's physical body to make it more likely that I will remember that I'm a Wanderer?"

"You can learn to enjoy silence."

"Come again? Do I have to learn to shut up?"

He laughed. "No. That would not be possible, or natural, for you. You can talk all you want. But sometime during your busy life you will want to sit in meditation."

"But I don't know how to meditate. Can you teach me now before I return?"

"I will teach you. But you must be taught again while you're in the physical body. You must be taught by a Master. That is very important. There is a new consciousness entering your society, new ideas. Many people call this New Age information. Much of it is useful. Much of it is confusing. The New Age movement speaks of many of the same things I speak of, but there are major differences between what I tell you and what you will find in most New Age books. I will go over these differences with you. Even if you don't remember them consciously while you're in the body, you will have a sense for what is true and that sense will guide you on your path. You will even write about the things I tell you now."

"I can't imagine that a story about a dragon could bring out any profound truths."

"It all depends on the dragon, Shari. Listen attentively to these points. Meditation is never an act of mood making. Pure silence, pure consciousness, the eternal side of your nature—it is beyond thought. You cannot talk yourself into it. It comes by grace and by grace alone. But what is grace? How do you make it come? That is where a Master is important. Many in the New Age movement are too anxious to throw off all authority. They say that no one can teach anything, that it is all inside the student. And that is true to a certain extent. On the other hand, to uncover what is inside you must bow at the feet of someone who has already discovered that great treasure. I use the word *bow* carefully. Because until a person is ready to humble himself and admit that he doesn't know, then he can learn nothing of value. It takes great humility to even approach a Master. These are things the New Age movement sometimes forgets."

"The whole eighteen years I was on Earth, I never saw a Master."

"This time you will. They will begin to appear in the world at this time. They teach techniques: meditation, certain kinds of breathing, physical exercises. But a technique only points toward the goal. It is not the goal itself. It is like a branch on a tree at nighttime. You can say to a friend, 'Follow the way that branch points and you will see the most wonderful star.' The branch gives direction, but it is not the same as the star. The branch is made of wood, the star is pure energy. Or say you want to eat a bowl of cereal. To do that you need the technique of using a spoon: how to hold it, which end to put in the bowl, how it goes up and into your mouth. The spoon is crucial, but it is the cereal you want. The cereal is the grace. Grace flows from a Master. It has to flow because he embodies that divine love."

"I wish I had been on Earth with you in Egypt," I said.

"You were. You are. You are with me there as much as you are with me now."

I shook my head. "Let's stick to one time frame, please, or I just end up confused."

"If you wish. But sometimes a Master is purposely confusing. He destroys preconceived ideas and beliefs. Always, though, he gives an aspirant a spiritual practice. That is very necessary to do even though many on the physical plane don't think so. They say, 'The time is changing and all will be taken care of.' They don't want to do any practice. And they are right, to a certain extent. The time is changing. That is why so many Wanderers are beginning to appear on Earth—to help prepare for this change. Mankind is entering a new age where spirituality will dominate. But many fear this change. They have heard about the disasters that are to come. Many so-called prophets say the majority of the world will be wiped out. That is not true. The world has an insurance policy. It has the Masters. There will be disasters, however, to shake things up a little. It can take a needle to remove a thorn. It can take a shaking of the Earth for people not to totally depend on the Earth, to make them look inside. You will write stories about the disasters as

Christopher Pike

well. People will read them and understand that when things appear the darkest, it is a sign that dawn is near. You will write stories of enlightened dragons and aliens, and people will want to learn to meditate. Even though the coming dawn is inevitable, it is good to be awake to enjoy it. Meditation helps with that."

"I am never going to remember all this," I said. "I can't remember half of what you just said."

"It doesn't matter. I see your mind has begun to wander. That is all right—you are a Wanderer, after all." He paused. "You want to see Peter."

I nodded. I knew I could hide nothing from the Rishi. "I miss him."

"Where would you like to see him?"

"What do you mean?"

The Rishi knelt for a moment and picked a red flower that resembled a rose. He gestured to the serene landscape. "I told you, this is all a dream. What would you like to dream with Peter? It can be anything. It can even be that you don't know that it is a dream. Really, that is all human life is. Just a dream people choose to enter into so that they can learn something. But people take it so seriously and become afraid of their own creation. They even fear to wake up. That is the one lesson humanity most needs to learn in the coming days. That there is no reason to be afraid. That things will work out for the best. That God knows what she's doing."

"She?"

He tapped me on the head with his flower. "When I am with you, Shari, you are my God. What universe do you wish to create for you and Peter?"

I considered. Boy did I consider. "It can be any-thing?"

"Anything."

I blushed; I could feel the blood in my cheeks even though I was a ghost. "Can it be an R-rated creation?"

"Yes."

"I don't want you to watch."

"I won't watch."

I laughed. "You promise?"

"I promise." He chuckled. "I swear it, Shari."

I rubbed my hands together in anticipation. "Awe-some. Let the creation begin. Let there be light. Let there be boys!"

I never knew I had such a dirty mind.

Well, I may have suspected.

CHAPTER
VI

*J*EAN RODRIGUES couldn't remember when she had last tied her little brother's shoes. Teddy sat above her on the kitchen table as she knelt at his feet and stared at her as if trying to remember the same thing. He was a cute four-year-old, with hair as long as a girl's and dimples. He touched the top of her head as she finished with his laces. She no longer wore her bandage, although she still suffered from a dull headache. But she couldn't complain; her ribs and knee were healed. She had been released from the hospital nine days earlier. She had just made it to her high school graduation the night before, and had been happy to be there. It was before nine on Saturday morning, two weeks after her fall.

"Is your head sore?" he asked.

She smiled and clasped his outstretched hand. "Now that you've touched it, Teddy, it's all better. Did you know you have magic hands?"

He blinked at her pronouncement and pulled his

hands back to study them. His eyes went wide. "What can they do?" he asked.

"They can give love. That is their special magic. Go give Mom a hug and then you go play. Here, I'll help you down."

Jean lifted Teddy from the table and he hurried over to the sofa where their mother lounged in front of the TV. Today was their mother's only day off. Teddy gave her the briefest of hugs before dashing out the door yelling something about showing the other kids his hands. They both laughed at him. Her mother shook her head.

"You'll have that boy trying to heal all the kids on the block, Jean," she said.

Jean sat beside her on the sofa. "Maybe he can," she said thoughtfully.

Her mother continued to smile. "I don't think anyone's sick around here at the moment."

"There's sick and there's sick," Jean muttered.

"What do you mean?"

Jean smiled quickly. "Nothing, just mumbling. Are you still worried about me being a candy striper? I won't go if it really upsets you."

"I think you're still too weak to be volunteering for a job that pays nothing."

"But if it did pay well, I would be strong enough?"

Her mother slapped her playfully on the arm with a magazine. "That's not what I mean and you know it. You should rest while you have the chance. Why did you tell the nurses you were coming in anyway? Is it so that you can see Lenny? You can see him without working."

"I do want to be close to Lenny, that's true. But I volunteered because when I was in the hospital I saw a lot of patients who weren't getting any attention because the nurses are too overworked." Jean shrugged. "I don't want to sound like a saint. I just want to help out."

Her mother stared at her. "But you do sound different."

Jean started to deny it, but only nodded. "Carol said the same thing. But I don't feel any different since the accident, except for my constant headache."

Her mother continued to watch her. "I don't believe that. You seem freer in a way. You don't walk around like you have the weight of the world on your shoulders."

"I never used to do that."

"Yes, you did. You were always *triste.*"

Jean shrugged again. "Well, maybe I had my reasons."

Her mother nodded. "Do you want to talk about it?"

"About what?"

"You know. Your pregnancy."

Jean acted shocked. "Was I pregnant? God, those comas are amazing things. Here I slept through an immaculate conception and a miscarriage all in the same two days."

"I was pregnant with you when I was your age," her mother said.

Jean quieted. "I know. I thought about that a lot."

"Before or after you had sex with Lenny?"

Jean looked over sharply. "Only after I failed the E.P.T."

"You took one of those? Where did you get one of those?"

"At the same drugstore where I bought the condoms that didn't work." Jean shook her head. "They're not hard to use. All you have to do is be able to pee in a tube." Jean paused. "Why are you asking me these questions, Mom? You must know Lenny doesn't stand a chance in hell of knocking me up again."

"I'm sorry what happened to him. You know I mean that. I'm sure he was a fine young man."

"He still is, Mama. Being crippled hasn't changed that. Not in my book."

Her mother touched her arm. "I'm going to say something harsh now, and you're not going to want to hear it. But I just want you to listen to me a second and think about it. I know Lenny is hurt and needs your help. You should go see him and help him in any way you can. But I think it would be a mistake for you not to see the facts for what they are. Lenny's going to be crippled for the rest of his life. At best he will be able to get around in a wheelchair. You can't let yourself get any more attached to him than you already are."

Jean spoke calmly. "Why not?"

"I just told you why. Because he's crippled for life. You can't be with a man like that. You'll spend all your time taking care of him."

A tear sprang into Jean's eye, but she managed to keep her expression flat. "I like taking care of people."

"No, you don't. You've never liked it before. You can't be with half a man."

Jean drew in a painful breath. "First you're worried that I was pregnant. Now you're worried I want to be with someone who can't get me pregnant. What's the deal, Mom?"

Her mother sighed. "Maybe this is not the time to talk about this. You go see him. Do what you can for him. We'll talk later."

Jean stood and looked down at her. "I'll feel the same later. I love him. I didn't know that before, even when I slept with him, but I know now. Maybe my love can't heal him. Maybe I just lied to Teddy and there isn't any magic in this world. But at least my love makes him whole in my eyes. Lenny is not half a man." She turned away. "Now, if you'll excuse me, I think I'll wait outside for Carol. She's supposed to pick me up in a few minutes."

Her mother sounded sad. "I don't want to fight with you, Jean. I just want to protect you."

Jean paused at the door. "I know that. We're not fighting. We're just—arguing." She opened the door. "Have a nice day, Mama. I don't know when I'll be home."

While waiting for Carol, Jean reflected on why those close to her were saying she had changed. There was truth in their comments. Despite Lenny's serious injury and her own wounds, she did feel lighter. Each morning she woke up anxious to start the day. Why, even the sun was brighter, the sky bluer. It was as if she had refound a childhood innocence she couldn't remember ever having enjoyed. Plus her head was filled with strange ideas she had never had before. She kept thinking of the stars and planets, dreaming of ancient civilizations, imagining vast supernatural dramas. She had begun to jot down her thoughts in a notebook, although she had no idea what she would do with them.

"What did happen that night?" she wondered aloud.

Carol arrived a few minutes later. She was on her way to a date with the Russian guy who worked at McDonald's, the guy with the scarred face. Seemed the guy didn't have a car. Carol was dressed to kill and excitedly smoking a joint. She offered Jean a hit the moment Jean got in the car. Jean took the joint and threw it in the garbage can at the end of their driveway.

"Hey!" Carol protested. "I just rolled that."

"I don't want any."

"Well, excuse me. I want it. You could have just said no and handed it back." Carol started to get out of the car. "I'm getting it."

Jean grabbed her arm and smiled. "I don't even want to have to smell it. Leave it in the can, *por favor.*"

Carol looked at her as if she were an alien creature. "You don't want to get loaded anymore? What's gotten into you?"

Jean let go of Carol and gestured to the block. "You see this street? There's graffiti on every wall. There's garbage on every lawn. Paint is peeling from the houses. Dogs and children are running wild. This is my street, but your street is just as bad."

"So? We live on the crappy side of town. When you get rich and famous, you can move to Malibu."

"I don't want to move to Malibu. I want to stay in this neighborhood because this is where I grew up. I want to clean up this place. I have given it a lot of thought. But I can't clean this place up by myself and, besides, it will just get dirty again because the minds of too many people around here are dirty. I know we get screwed in school. We have the worst teachers and the ugliest buildings. I know we get screwed at work because we're not white. But I think we're screwing ourselves with all the drugs we're taking. Look, you and I have been stoned since we were twelve. Haven't you gotten sick of it yet?"

Carol stared at her dumbfounded. "I don't know. I guess."

"I'm sick of it. I'm not getting loaded again, ever."

"But you'll still smoke pot now and then, won't you?"

"Carol. I'm not taking anything. And I don't want you to, either."

Carol was annoyed. "Right, great. If I don't want to be Miss Purity, I can't be your friend anymore. You know it, Jean, you might be nicer nowadays, but you're also turning into a royal pain in the ass."

"I didn't say you couldn't be my friend anymore. It's just that every time you light up a joint around me, I'm going to throw it away. And you won't be able to stop me 'cause I can kick your ass any day." Jean smiled sweetly. "But I still love you, Carol."

Carol put the car in gear. "Thank God for that."

They headed for the hospital. The day was hot and Carol's air-conditioning hadn't worked since the last ice age. Jean rolled down her window and looked at the houses she had seen every day of her life. Somehow, it was as if she were seeing them for the first time. It was true, most of them were in poor shape, but Jean could see the potential there. Everywhere she looked, she saw all kinds of possibilities.

"How long are you working at the hospital?" Carol asked.

"Three hours. That's all they'll let me with my injuries, and I had to push for those."

"Why are you doing it?"

"So I can steal hospital drugs."

"But you just said you don't want to get loaded anymore?"

Jean laughed. *"Menso!* See what all that *mota* has done to your brain? I'm not going to steal drugs. I volunteered to work at the hospital because they need help. That's the only reason."

Carol was impressed. "That's neat. Maybe you'll get to give some way-cool girl or guy a shot in the ass."

Jean couldn't stop laughing. "They don't let candy stripers give shots. Certainly not to way-cool girls and guys."

"Well, I don't know what they do."

"Tell me what's happening with you? Why are you going out with a guy?"

"He's not exactly normal, you know."

"I understand that. But he is a he. That makes him different from a girl."

Carol giggled. "That's true."

"Look, are you still a lesbian or not? I just want to know for future reference. If you're not, then I can quit defending you."

"Does it bother you to defend me?" Carol asked.

"No. It turns me on. But answer my question."

"I don't know the answer. I just know I like this guy.

73

But I still like girls. Maybe I'm bisexual." Carol paused. "Does that gross you out?"

"No," Jean said honestly. "It makes you complex. I like that in a boy or a girl."

Carol nodded. "I like to think it gives me color."

"Just remember that a guy can get you pregnant where a girl can't."

"I have you to remind me of that." Carol paused. "Will you get to help Lenny today?"

Jean sighed. "I don't know if I can help Lenny. I've seen him every day since I woke up, but he hardly talks to me. I keep thinking he'll feel better when the bones in his back have healed enough so he can start physical therapy. Lying in bed all day would depress anybody."

"When will he be able to get into a wheelchair?"

"Not for a while. Another couple of months."

"That long?"

"At least. Where his back broke, they had to fuse the spine together. That takes time to heal."

"Will he ever walk again?" Carol asked.

Jean hesitated. "The traditional medical answer is no. That's the answer he's supposed to learn to accept. But I don't believe it. I can't help but think his condition is only temporary." She shook her head. "Maybe I'm just fooling myself."

"I hope he gets better. Hey, have you seen Darlene lately?"

"No. She never talks to me. She never came to visit me at the hospital. What's with her?"

"I think she still plans to go after Juan," Carol said.

"After all that's happened? You can't be serious."

Jean was thoughtful. "I'd like to talk to her more about what happened that night Lenny and I got hurt. You know, weird as this may sound, I don't even know if she was still there when we fell."

"I think she was," Carol said. "I think she's the one who called the ambulance."

"But you're not sure?"

"No. What does Lenny say?"

"That he can't remember."

"Do you believe him?" Carol asked.

Jean shrugged. "I don't know why he'd lie to me." She added, "We can't let Darlene go after Juan. It would be a death sentence for her."

Carol looked worried. "Maybe for all of us."

Carol dropped Jean off at the hospital twenty minutes later. She was going to spend the day with Scarface, and Jean assured her she could take the bus home. Actually, Jean liked riding the bus, especially since her accident. It was a good place to meet people.

Her candy-striper duties were simple: she delivered meals to patients. But even this job turned out to be complex with the elderly patients. Not one but two old women thought she was their granddaughter. At first Jean denied the relationship, but when she saw how much it meant to the women to have a visit from a granddaughter, Jean decided to play along, reminiscing about events she had no memory of and adding details the women had no minds to doubt. On the whole she had the most fun with the senior citizens and children. Really, helping people got her high, and somehow she had known it would happen.

The patient who affected her the most, though, was a teenage girl named Debra Zimmerer. She was eighteen, the same as Jean, and dying. Just before Jean delivered her food, the nurses told her that Debra had leukemia, and they felt she wasn't going to make it. When Jean brought in her tray, she found Debra lying in bed and reading J.R.R. Tolkien's *The Lord of the Rings,* which Jean had read in the hospital. Debra was worn-out pretty, with faded brown eyes as weary as those of a sick model in an old oil painting. She was five feet five and weighed maybe eighty pounds. Jean took one look at her and felt a painful stab in her gut, but somehow she managed to smile as she set down the tray.

"Awesome book, huh?" Jean asked.

Debra set the fat book aside. "I guess. I'm just near the beginning."

"Keep going. It keeps getting better and better. In fact, I think it's the best story I ever read." Jean lifted the lid off her plate. "Would you like something to eat? I brought you chicken, but if you don't like it they have some kind of fish."

Debra sat up weakly. "I'm not that hungry."

"How about something to drink? I have apple juice or orange juice or ginger ale."

Debra nodded. "I could drink some ginger ale."

Jean opened the can and poured Debra a glass. Debra's voice was dry, which Jean understood to be a side effect of the morphine she took to control the pain. Debra lifted it to her lips and took a sip. The act seemed to exhaust her, and she put down the glass quickly. Jean sat on the bed beside her.

"Is there anything else I can get you?" Jean asked.

Debra coughed. "No."

Jean patted her on the back. "Are you OK?"

Debra nodded and wiped at her colorless lips. "Yes."

Jean shook her head. "That was a stupid question. I'm sorry, of course you're not OK." She paused. "I heard you have leukemia."

Debra watched her. "Yes. It's a drag. What's your name?"

"Jean. You're Debra, right?"

"Yes." Debra glanced at the book. "Could you tell me how the story ends?"

Jean forced a smile. "I don't want to do that. It'll spoil it for you." Then she stopped, hearing what Debra was really asking her. It was a long story, really three books in one. Debra was not going to live long enough to finish it and she knew it. "But if you want me to, I can. I can do it today after I finish delivering these trays."

Debra stared at the far wall for a moment. "How about tomorrow? That would be a good day for me."

Jean nodded. "I can come tomorrow evening and tell you the whole story." She added, without even thinking about what she was going to say, "Maybe I can tell you one of my stories as well."

Debra was interested. "Do you write stories?"

Jean shrugged. "I'm only working on one so far. It's about this famous writer and her muse. Only her muse is a troll who appears out of her bedroom closet one day and demands half her royalties. I'll tell you what I have of it so far and you can tell me whether you think I should bother finishing it."

"OK." Debra lowered her head. "It'll be nice to have a visitor."

"Doesn't anyone come to see you?"

"Just my father. But I can't talk to him because he's too scared about me being sick." Debra hesitated. "He's afraid I'm going to die."

Jean spoke gently. "Are you afraid?"

Debra raised her head and wiped her nose. "Yeah. I know it's going to happen, but I'm still scared. My doctor told me." Again she stared at the far wall. "I have no idea what it's going to be like." She shrugged. "Maybe it won't be like anything. Maybe I'll just be dead and that will be it."

"No," Jean said firmly. "Your body will die but you'll go on."

Debra smiled sadly. "I wish I had your faith."

It was Jean's turn to hesitate because she really didn't know what she wanted to say to the poor girl. But at the same time she felt compelled to speak, and she believed that what she would say would be the truth.

"It's not that I have faith. I just *know* that your time of death is no more important than when you change your clothes. Don't ask me how I know. I can't explain it. The main thing is, when death comes, you don't need to be afraid. That's important. Fear is the only thing that can hold you back."

Debra listened. "Hold you back from what?"

"From going on to more joy. It's a lot harder to be born than to die. You'll see, and when you do, you'll say to yourself, 'That foolish girl in the hospital was right.'"

"Are you a fool?"

"Sure. But you know, only fools get into heaven."

Debra grinned. "Who told you that?"

Jean stood up quickly from the bed. Debra's question had a profound effect on her. For a moment Jean felt as if there were two of her standing in the room, one visible, the other a reflection. She felt as if she should be able to glance over her shoulder and see her other half to answer Debra's question. She felt inexplicable joy even with a dying girl watching her.

"Someone wise," Jean said softly, turning away. "I'll see you tomorrow."

"I hope so," Debra said with feeling.

It was inevitable that when she finished her shift Jean would go and stand at the end of Lenny's bed and try to think of something inspiring to say. Lenny had been moved to a normal room with the motorized bed that allowed him to be rotated without the assistance of four nurses. At present, thankfully, he was lying faceup and she was able to address him rather than his scarred back. Unfortunately, no words of wisdom came to her and he had yet to open his eyes despite her saying his name several times. She heard her mother's words in her mind and had to convince herself they weren't true.

"I can leave if you want me to," Jean said finally. "But you're going to have to tell me to leave. Otherwise I'll just stand here feeling awful. But maybe that's what you want, Lenny, I don't know."

He opened his eyes. "You should know by now what I want."

Jean stepped closer, touching his bare arm. This room, like his previous one, was warmer than normal. Probably because they kept him scantily dressed to make it easier to care for him.

"What do you want?" she asked reluctantly.

"To die," he said flatly.

There was anguish in her voice. "No."

"Yes." Finally he looked at her face. "I can't live like this. You say you love me, Jean. If you do, then help me end this."

She clasped his right hand. "You just have to hold on for a little while longer. Soon you'll be in a wheelchair and able to get out. I'll take you to the beach. I'll take you to the movies. You can't imagine how many great films have come out since you've been in here. I can show you—"

"You can take me," he interrupted. *"You* can show me. That's true because I can't do any of those things without you. But how long will you be there? You say forever but we both know that's B.S. One day you'll get tired of pushing a cripple around and you'll meet some other guy and then you'll say, 'I'm sorry Lenny but you know it's a tough world.' Then you'll leave, and what'll I do? I'll tell you. I'll kill myself. But why should I have to wait for the day we both know is going to come? I don't want to go through the pain. I want to do it now. I want you to help me."

Jean wept. "I won't leave you, I swear to you."

Lenny strained to move his head as close to hers as he could. "You can get what you want if you keep your eyes open and move fast. A bottle of sleeping pills, a dozen packaged shots of Demerol—either of these would be enough to kill me. Are you listening to me, Jean? If you don't help me you just make it harder for me. I'll have to slit my wrists. No, that will be too slow. I'll have to cut my throat. The blood will be all over the place. You'll walk in here one day and the walls will be sprayed with red and—"

"*Cállate!*" she cried.

Lenny let his head fall back. "I'm going to do it. You know I'm going to do it."

She sighed, her tears sprinkling his arm. "You must have some reason to live."

"None."

"Don't say that."

"I want to die today."

"Lenny."

"Right now."

"Damn you! You have to give yourself time. If you can't think of a reason to live, then you have to find one. Think, Lenny, of everything and everyone in the world. Think of something you want to do. Hold on to that, at least until you get out of here." She squeezed his hand, a desperate note in her voice. "Can't you think of anything?"

He started to answer but then stopped, only staring at her for several seconds. His expression became strangely blank. "Maybe," he muttered.

She nodded. "Good. That's a start. Hold on to that. It can make you strong."

"Don't you want to know what it is?" he asked.

She shook her head. "No. It doesn't matter. As long as it keeps you alive."

Lenny sucked in a weary breath and closed his eyes.

"But the day it stops doing that, then what? Will you help me end it?"

Her head throbbed. "Do I have to?"

"Yes. You must promise me."

She let go of his hand, let his arm drop. "I promise," she whispered.

CHAPTER
VII

*J*EAN DID NOT take the bus home after she left the hospital, but rather, to the beach, Huntington Beach, located in Orange County. It was a long ride for her, and on the way she kept asking herself why she was going there when Santa Monica Beach or Venice Beach was closer and just as nice. Indeed, she couldn't even remember when she had last entered Orange County. Yet a wave of nostalgia spread over her as the bus headed for the Huntington pier. Staring at the brightly colored shops, she felt strangely at home, at peace even. She was glad she had hours of free time. The dull ache of her perpetual headache had eased somewhat.

Jean had forty dollars on her. The first thing she did after getting off the bus was buy herself a bathing suit, a navy blue single piece affair that showed her breasts and bottom to good advantage. She wanted to look sexy but she also wanted something comfortable to swim in. She also bought herself a beach bag and towel and headed for the sand with the suit on. The area immediately around the pier looked like the happening place; she found a spot in the shade of the first lifeguard station. The people around her seemed so different from those in her neighborhood, she thought, with their rich summer attire and perfect hair. Most of the kids looked like they were riding their daddy's credit card limits. Yet, at the same time they were young and confused like everyone else she knew. She couldn't take her eyes off them. Since her accident she was always observing and watching, like a spectator at a play she had no part in.

Jean did not spend long lying on the sand. Soon she was in the water, and the motion of the waves was more than enough to wash away the stress of the last two weeks. She had always been an excellent swimmer. Her worries about Lenny and Debra fell off as she swam out three hundred yards past the first break and let herself bob up and down on the huge south swells. The air was hot, the water cool, and there wasn't a cloud in the sky. It was almost as if she swam in paradise.

Wherever I am is paradise because I am there. I am joy itself.

Where had she heard that? From a book? A teacher at school? She couldn't remember and it didn't matter because it was true, she was that joy, and that was all that mattered. She swam farther out and felt the ocean welcome her. The blue horizon seemed to stretch to infinity and she felt as if she could keep going. She felt completely free.

Then she began to feel tired. The fatigue came on her all at once, and when she turned and saw that the beach was a half mile back, she felt a stab of anxiety. The water felt cold now. She wasn't out of the hospital that long. Her supposedly healed ribs suddenly didn't feel as if they were all knitted together. What if she cramped up? She might die. Yet it wasn't the thought of death that frightened her. It was the idea that she'd leave without completing an important task. For the first time in her life Jean felt she was on Earth for a purpose.

She slowly began to make her way back in, conserving her strength as best she could. She was halfway to the beach and experiencing exhaustion when the lifeguard boat happened by. The twenty-five-year-old-bronze god behind the wheel waved and asked if she'd like a ride to the shore. She humbled herself and gasped that she would. Once aboard, the lifeguard complimented her on her stamina and her bathing suit. But he didn't hit on her or anything. He probably rescued way-cool babes all day, she thought. His name was Ken, as in Barbie and Ken. He kind of looked like Ken.

The warm sand was a delicious treat for her weary goose-bump-covered limbs. She lay back on her towel and was out in ten seconds. She slept for an hour, and dreamt of the sun and the heavens. She flew above mankind's burning star on the back of an angel, while all worlds spun below her. Worlds of light, worlds of pain—it was all there for her to choose, the angel said. If she wished to go back.

"Go back," Jean whispered as she awakened with a start. She sat up and looked around, feeling as if she had to start back. But not to the other side of town, to her side of town. But to another place, she thought.

She stood and collected her towel and clothes. Without knowing why, almost as if in a dream, she walked north.

Two miles from the pier, on a stretch of sand where Huntington Beach ended and Bolsa Chica Beach began, a row of expensive and multistoried condominiums had been erected to provide a view of Catalina on every clear day Southern California had to offer. Jean paused to stare at them. It was not their decor that drew her—if anything she thought they were something of an eyesore, with their oversize balconies protruding from their back sides like lines drawn on a blueprint by an architect on acid. She realized she had a prejudice against places she knew she'd never be able to afford. Still, the condos drew her attention, even though she didn't like them, even though they frightened her. How curious, she thought, to fear buildings she had never seen before. Yet it was as if the condos were bathed in black and red light, in memories of horror that someone had desperately tried to blot out.

"But I've never been here before," Jean muttered to herself.

Horror can attract as well as repel. She felt herself walking toward the buildings, pulled by invisible strings that could have stretched from the ground as well as from the sky. She continued to move as if in a dream, her angel long gone, replaced by a being from a lower region who whispered silently. Maybe it was a demon, she thought. Maybe it was just someone's past that had somehow passed by without touching her.

The condo on the right, in particular, drew her. It was three stories high, like the others, but somehow it appeared taller. The roof was covered with orange clay adobe-style tiles. A metal fence surrounded the building, but the gate was open. Without asking permission, without ringing a bell, she went inside.

She went straight to the spot.

What spot? She didn't know what to call it. A stain on the ground.

Going down on her knees, she touched the dark stain on the smooth concrete and wondered what had made it? Why did it fill her with such dread? Who had died here?

Yes. That's the real question. It's a bloodstain, I can see that. Only blood permanently turns concrete dark. Only blood refuses to fade. Only blood never forgets.

Jean felt her hair slip forward over her shoulders and fall on to the stain. It was almost as if the strands of hair strained to soak up the blood that had once flowed at her knees. Soak it back into her head, deep into her brain cells, suffuse them with the life and death of that night. Whatever had happened here, she knew, had happened in the dark. It had been an act of surprise, an act of vengeance. Jean could feel all those things as she knelt there. But most of all she felt sorrow. Whoever had died here, she knew, had come to a bitter end.

Jean didn't know how long she remained by the stain. But eventually she became aware of a shadow stretching over her from above. She raised her eyes into the glare of the sun and saw a tall elderly lady in a lovely white dress. She carried a smart gray handbag in her right hand and it was obvious she had just had her hair done. Although she was as old as some of the patients Jean fed in the hospital, she was nowhere near retirement. She stood erect and her blue eyes were clear and alert.

"Can I help you, miss?" she asked in a pleasant voice.

Jean stood reluctantly. The stain repulsed her, while at the same time she was afraid to leave it. Somehow, it connected her to a part of herself she felt she should know. She wiped her palms over her knees—the heat of the concrete had slightly burned her flesh. She still had her suit on.

"No," Jean said, realizing how foolish she'd sound if she spoke of how the stain preyed on her mind. She stooped to collect her bag. "I was just resting. I'll be on my way."

"The way you were kneeling there," the woman said. "The expression on your face—I thought you knew her."

Jean stopped. "Knew who?"

The woman nodded to the stain. "The girl who died here."

Jean felt dizzy. She had to stick out her arm and hold on to a fence to support herself. "Oh, God," she whispered.

The woman put her hand on her arm to steady her. "Are you all right, dear?"

Jean nodded weakly. "Yes, I'm fine. It's just—the heat." She straightened up as well as she could, although the world continued to wobble as if the Huntington Beach fault had just decided to try for the top of the Richter scale. She added, "I really should be going," and turned in the direction of the gate but didn't move.

"If you'd like a glass of lemonade before you go, I'd be happy to get you one." The woman stuck out her hand. "My name's Rita Wilde. I manage several of the condos on this block. Most are owner occupied but quite a few are rentals."

Jean shook her hand. Her eyes kept straying back to the mark on the ground. "You were the manager here when the girl died?" Jean asked.

"Yes. It happened a year ago. She was about your age." Rita cocked her head upward. "She fell off that balcony right above us." Rita frowned. "She might have lived if she hadn't landed directly on her head."

"How did she fall?"

A shadow crossed Rita's face. "A bunch of teenagers were having a party. The parents weren't home. The girl didn't die until near the end of the party. At first everyone thought she jumped. But then the police figured out she had been shoved. It was all over the papers. You must have read about it."

"I didn't. Not that I remember at least." Jean nodded to the stain. "This is from where she hit the ground?"

"Yes. I've tried a dozen times to scrub it away but it refuses to go. The poor child. She was only eighteen."

"I'm eighteen," Jean said quickly.

Rita smiled. "Are you? That's a wonderful age. What I wouldn't give to be eighteen again. Can I get you that glass of lemonade now?"

"No, that's OK. I'm feeling a bit better." Jean hesitated. "Do you remember the girl's name?"

Rita stopped to scratch her head. "It was something

Cooper. I can't remember her first name. But I do know her parents lived near Adams. The father came by a couple of days after she died. I talked to him and he told me a little about himself." Rita shrugged. "I guess he just wanted to see the spot where his daughter had died. Maybe I'd do the same, I don't know." Rita paused and studied her. "Are you sure you weren't friends with that girl?"

Cooper. Adams. Cooper. The father. Cooper.

The words chilled Jean to the bone.

"No," Jean said. "I didn't know her. Why do you ask?"

It was Rita's turn to look at the stain. "I don't know. It's just a thought I had."

Jean began to back away. "Thank you for your time, Rita. Have a nice day."

"You, too, child. Enjoy yourself."

Jean searched for a telephone booth the moment she left the complex. She found one outside on a liquor store wall a block over. There was a telephone book; she hastily scanned the white pages and found sixteen Coopers. She flipped to the map at the front of the book and located Adams, studied the streets around it, then returned to the list of sixteen. Only one man, Stewart Cooper on Delaware, lived anywhere near Adams. She memorized his number and again consulted the map. From where she stood it was approximately three miles to the man's house, but she figured she would probably have to walk half that distance just to catch the bus home. She decided to pay Mr. Cooper a visit.

But what are you going to say to him? I didn't know

your daughter but I'm sorry she's dead. And, oh, by the way, her bloodstain really freaked me out. When my hair fell on it, I felt as if I were the one who had died. Imagine that?

Jean decided to cross that bridge when she came to it. She entered the liquor store and bought herself a tall Coke. Her walk already had her dehydrated. Taking a couple of slugs from the bottle, she set out for Adams, this time heading south, back toward the pier. She figured it would take her close to an hour to reach the Cooper residence. Plenty of time for her to figure out what the hell she was doing.

As it turned out, her estimate was overly optimistic. Between her long swim and her still healing body, she couldn't do twenty-minute miles. She was about to call a cab by the time she stumbled onto Delaware, *ninety* minutes later. Fortunately the Cooper house wasn't far up from the beach. In fact, it's just over there, she thought. The house with the white picket fence and the maple in front. . . .

Wait a second! I have to check the address to know which house it is. I don't know anything about picket fences and maple trees. Hell, I couldn't tell a maple tree from an olive tree, even if it was growing maples.

That was true, she thought. But what was also true was that she recognized the house the instant she saw it. She didn't have to confirm her feeling by checking the number she'd obtained from the phone book. The Cooper house was the third house on the right. Still, as she drew closer, she did check the number against the numbers on the curb. The perfect match brought another wave of dizziness to her already overwhelmed brain. As did the sight of the young man in the driveway loading his pickup. He was tall and handsome with dark hair and a nice build and that was cool and everything. But what was not so cool, at least not at the moment, was that he looked so familiar.

He, in fact, looked like someone she had known all her life.

Yet she had never seen him before.

"He's the dead girl's brother," she whispered to herself.

Jean walked up to him, probably looking like the overheated radiator that she felt like. His truck was loaded with a disassembled bed and a chest of drawers, plus a generous helping of wrinkled clothes and what appeared to be a PC. It didn't take a genius to realize he was moving out. He had a gold-colored lamp in his hand when he glanced over at her. His eyes were warm and blue and yet they sent a shiver down to her toes.

"Can I help you?" he asked.

"Yes," she mumbled. "Which way is the beach?"

He pointed toward the large blue body of water at her back, the one with the waves and the salt in it, and the sandy beach beside it. "It's over there," he said.

She glanced over her shoulder. "Oh, yeah. I have a terrible sense of direction."

"You're not from around here?" he asked. The way he spoke, she knew he knew the answer to his own question—which he should have, because of her inner-city bad-girl accent. Yet, even though she liked him, she didn't like being categorized. She straightened up and cleared her throat.

"How can you tell?" she asked.

He shrugged and set down his lamp. "Your voice. Your bathing suit."

"What's wrong with my bathing suit? I just bought it. I bought it down here."

He paused and studied her up and down, perhaps wondering what he was getting himself into, and if it was worth it. "There's nothing wrong with it," he said carefully. "It just doesn't look like the kind of suit girls around here wear."

"Because my ass doesn't stick out?"

He smiled. "If you like. Where are you from?"

Jean took a step closer to him. "Guess."

"South Central."

"Close enough. Does that scare you?"

"Well, since it doesn't look as if you're carrying a switchblade or a gun beneath that suit, I'd have to say no."

"I might have one in my bag. You never know."

He gestured to his jammed truck. "If you are going to rob me, these are all the worldly possessions I have. Take what you want, I don't care."

Jean smiled. "I'm not as dangerous as I look. Are you moving out or is that a stupid question?"

He nodded. "Yeah, it's finally time to leave the nest. I found a studio apartment up on Baker. It's on the third floor. There's a pool, but the place is kind of small. But then I don't have a lot of stuff."

"Did you move that chest of drawers by yourself?"

"Yeah."

"I'm not impressed. That's a good way to wreck your back. Isn't any of your family home to help you?"

"There's just my mom and dad, and I want to move

93

while they're out." He shook his head thoughtfully. "My mother isn't exactly crazy about me leaving."

"Is it because you're their only child?"

He hesitated. "Yeah. There are just the three of us."

Jean offered her hand. "My name's Jean Rodrigues. What's yours?"

"James Cooper." He shook her hand. "Pleased to meet you."

It was weird to touch him. It was like touching a mirror, while an old friend stood behind her. "I bet people call you Jimmy," she said.

Her remark made him stiffen. "Not usually. Most people just call me Jim."

"Then that's what I'll call you." She nodded to the truck. "It looks like you're about ready to take this load over. I'll give you a hand if you like."

Her offer took him aback. But then he smiled. "That's nice of you. But you're dressed for the beach. You should just go and enjoy yourself."

"I have an ulterior motive in wanting to help you, Jim. I took the bus over here and it'll take me two hours to get home. If I help you move your stuff, then I was thinking maybe you could give me a ride home." She added, "You're going to need some help if your place is on the third floor."

He raised his eyebrows at her offer. She could see he was shy, a sweet guy. By the faint lines around his eyes, she could also see that he had suffered in his life. It had to do with his sister, she knew. Yet she didn't feel this was the time to ask about her.

"Can you work in a bathing suit?" he asked finally.

"Are you afraid my breasts might pop out?"

He blushed. "I wasn't worried about that exactly."

"I have clothes in my bag here, along with my forty-four Magnum." She paused. "I would like to help you."

He watched her. "Why, Jean?"

She smiled. "Because I'm grateful to you. You showed me where the ocean is."

CHAPTER

VIII

I LIVED IN THE REALITY of my own creation. I had put on my memory cap, however, and didn't know that I was both my own God and devil. I was Shari Cooper and I was alive on planet Earth and back in high school. It was my sophomore year and at the moment nothing was more important than Peter Nichols asking me to the prom. I could see him approaching in the crowded hallway. My heart pounded like a piston in my chest when he smiled at me.

"Shari," he said. "How are you doing?"

My hands were filled with school books and I worried they would be ruined with the sweat pouring off my palms. Peter looked so good then, his curly blond hair hanging in his blue eyes. Standing so cool in the hustle and bustle of the break between first and second period. Like he had just pitched nine innings of no-hit ball in the World Series and was about to be handed the MVP award.

"Great," I said. "How are you?"

"Cool. Going to the prom tomorrow night?"

"Maybe."

"Why maybe?"

I shrugged like it was no big deal. "Haven't got a date yet."

"Do you want to go with me?" he asked.

I managed to hold on to my books. "Sure."

"What time should I pick you up?"

"How about six?"

"Six is good." He patted me on the back and stepped past me. "See you then."

Wow, I thought. Peter Jacobs. What a guy. Shari and Peter. What a couple.

Then it was Friday night, just like that, and I was upstairs finishing my hair and the doorbell rang. The noise startled me; my brush handle broke off in my hand, the bristles in my hair. But I just laughed; I was high as a kite. I ran down the stairs to find my mother and father opening the door for Peter. My father pumped his hand and my mother gave him a quick hug. They liked Peter, of course. He was a winner. He was my fastball. I was hoping for some fast times tonight as I hurried toward him. His tux was the color of sand on an ocean floor. He smiled at me and handed me a corsage as large and as white as the moon.

"You look great, Shari," he said.

"Thank you." I accepted the corsage. "You don't look so bad yourself."

My parents stood nearby and beamed happily.

We drove to the prom in a silver limo that Peter had rented. The dinner and dance were in the same expensive hotel. There was steak and lobster, music and candles. We danced long and slow and Peter put his arms around me and told me how much he cared for me. I whispered the same. A vote was taken on fancy folded cards and not long after Peter and I were crowned "Coolest Couple." The band played us a special song—"Stairway to Heaven." I felt as if I had died and gone to heaven. And the night was still young. Peter kissed my ear and told me he had rented a room upstairs. Did I want to see it? Sure, I said. If that's what he wanted. He nodded and took my hand and we strode toward the elevator, while all my girlfriends watched in envy.

The suite was plush. There were flowers, a bottle of champagne on ice, soft music on the stereo. We drank a toast to ourselves. Then Peter kissed me and led me into the bedroom. The light was down low. He began to undress me.

"Do you want to make love?" he asked softly.

"Yes. Yes. Do you?"

"Yes," he said. "Help me get out of these clothes."

"I love you, Peter," I said as I unbuttoned his shirt.

"I love you, Shari."

I opened his shirt and rubbed my palm over his hard muscles.

A metallic-colored monster burst out of the center of his chest.

"Eehhh!" I screamed and leapt back. In horror, I watched as Peter toppled to the floor, his blood and guts splattering the carpet. The monster climbed out of his ruined cavity and stood upright. Its head was enormous. As it peered at me, its mouth opened and a band of razor-sharp teeth protruded and snapped at the air. In the space of seconds it grew to eight feet tall. Too numb to shout for help, I backed into the corner and tried to be invisible. But the monster was hungry and wanted prime California girl flesh. Slowly it moved toward me, acid slime dripping from its mouth and burning the carpet. It would use the acid to digest me, I knew. I had maybe three seconds left alive. At last I found my throat and let out a bloodcurdling scream.

The monster stopped and peered at me curiously. It spoke in Peter's voice.

"Did I scare you?" he asked.

I was about to faint. "What?" I gasped.

"It's me, Peter," the alien said.

I frowned. "Is that a costume?" I pointed to his dead body. "What the hell is going on here?"

"We're at the prom," he said. "This is supposed to be the night of our lives."

I was having trouble taking it all in. "But are you inside that monster, Peter? It looks so real."

"Oh, it's real enough." It turned its huge head back toward Peter's body. "You want to see it eat what's left of me?"

"No!" I cried. "Get out of that suit now. You're making me sick to my stomach." I was suddenly angry. "I didn't like being scared like that. You almost gave me a heart attack."

"I couldn't have done that to you."

"No, I'm serious. I almost had a heart attack."

The monster sat down on the floor. "You can't have a heart attack, Shari. Don't you remember? You're dead."

It all came back to me in an instant. Then I was really pissed. I strode over and whacked the monster on the head. "We both agreed to block our memories.

We were supposed to go to the prom like it was real. Since when have you known this was all make-believe?"

"Since it started."

"That's not fair! Here I'm swooning under your attention and you're sitting in your fat head and chuckling at me. That's it, that's the last romantic fantasy I'm acting out with you. I'm going to find some other ghost. Maybe an Englishman from the last century. Those guys were supposed to have manners. I'm really angry at you, Peter."

The alien shrugged. "Sorry. I didn't mean to hold on to my memory. It just happened. Then as the night dragged on I started to get bored. I just wanted to liven things up."

"Oh, thank you! I feel much better now! You get to go to the prom with me and screw me afterward and you're bored. Thanks a lot Mr. MVP."

"We didn't exactly screw afterward."

"We were about to. Why did you choose that moment to have an alien burst out of your chest? Do you know what that does for my self-esteem?"

"You're not supposed to have self-esteem problems."

"Why not?"

"You don't have a body for one thing."

"So? I'm still a person. I'm still walking around in the image of the body I had on Earth."

"Why?"

I stopped. "Why what?"

"Why don't you switch to another body?"

"What's wrong with this one? Is that why you got bored tonight? I wasn't cute enough for you? God, I'm happy I didn't date you when I was alive. I would have ended up killing myself. And would you get out of that stupid alien form? You really are making me sick. Not that the sight of your old self probably won't do the same thing."

The monster vanished, as did Peter's dead body. He stood before me as I had met him at my funeral, wearing blue jeans and a baseball cap. "I just wanted to experiment is all," he said. "You don't have to get all bent out of shape."

I sighed. "I suppose not. It's just that I never got to go to the prom with you. I dreamed about it so much and this seemed like a good chance to have a dream come true. You can understand that, can't you?"

Peter put an arm around me, and in that moment it felt pretty real to me, and wonderful, his touch, like the touch of my oldest and best friend. I was still having trouble with all this consciousness business but I supposed the Rishi would explain it to me more if I asked. Once again I was glad he had promised not to observe my fantasy life. He was so wise—I didn't want to act the fool in front of him.

"We can do it again, Shari," Peter said. "We can start from when I asked you out. This time, I promise, I'll have my memory blocked. We can even have sex if you want."

I looked at him. "If *I* want? Don't you want?"

He shrugged. "Sure."

"What does that mean? Has being dead affected you more than you've let on?"

He took a step back. "Are you asking me if I'm impotent?"

"It's nothing to be ashamed of if you are. We can talk about it."

Peter was bored. "Shari, think for a second. How can I be impotent when I can sprout a dozen tentacles and talons in two seconds and eat you alive if I want to?"

I paused. "I see your point. Never mind."

"Do you want to start the date over?"

I paced the hotel room. "No. I want to do something more meaningful. Let's go exploring. The Rishi said we could go anywhere we wanted in the universe just by wishing it. I've always wanted to see the solar system. Interested?"

Peter smiled. Such a lovely boy and smile. "Always," he said.

We hung suspended above planet Earth, seeing it as astronauts, and more. For our eyes were sensitive to colors and feelings ordinary humans failed to perceive. I saw that the Earth had both a physical and spiritual dimension. Much of the Middle East, for example, was clean desert covered with dark astral clouds. Intuitively I understood the darkness was from the constant strife there, and that the area could not go on the way it had been and survive. While other parts of the Earth shone with soft white radiance. The Himalayas in India, in particular, were beautiful to behold, and the West Coast of America also had some points of brilliance, as did a few other spots on the globe. But it saddened me to see that the lights were few compared to the darkness.

"Too bad *Time* magazine never had a picture of the

Earth like this on their front cover," I said to Peter, who floated beside me.

"It is strange to see that hate is something you *can* see," he agreed. He pointed to the Middle East. "I do hope they get their act together there. It looks ready to explode."

"I feel that way, too. It's almost as if it would take an explosion to break the tension there."

"Or a huge wave of light," Peter said.

I nodded thoughtfully. "That would be preferable."

"Well, there's nothing we can do about it right now. Where would you like to go next?"

I turned around, seeing an old friend behind me. "Let's go to the Moon!"

There was no obvious sensation of speed as we soared toward Earth's natural satellite: no wind in our hair, no roar of a rocket engine. Yet the flight was exhilarating. Having the Moon rush steadily toward me, I never felt so free, so possessed by the certainty that all this was indeed my creation, as much as everybody else's, a playground made for all of us by God to learn in and enjoy. With a simple thought, I slowed as we neared the silver globe. But Peter was having too much fun and rammed headfirst into the Moon. We danced about on a crater-marked field, and then were off again, heading for the fourth planet from the sun, the red planet. Mysterious Mars.

Here I discovered both wonder and fear. On a purely physical level Mars appeared uninhabited, but studying it with the spiritual eye I was learning to use, I was treated to two interlocking visions. On what I can only describe as a low vibration, I saw a race of demonic reptilian beings. A cruel civilization that fought and warred with itself and every other living being in its dimension. Here there was no light, no love, and as a result, only pain. I could only tune into it for a few seconds before being forced to shut it out.

"Do you see it?" I asked Peter.

He nodded gravely. "It's like hell. Yet it's there with the other as well. How can that be? Two races on one world and our scientists on Earth can see neither."

"I think there's a lot that science has yet to learn." I focused on the other race. I say focused only in a manner of speaking. Actually, I found I could perceive more by "letting go" inside. Several octaves above the reptilians were enchanted cities of beings who looked similar to people on Earth. Immediately I was reminded of the haunting civilization the author Ray Bradbury had described in his book *The Martian Chronicles.* For these were a beautiful people with long shiny gowns, wine-colored faces, and sleek bodies. Canals filled with luminous dark liquids crisscrossed their globe and they floated from town to town along these watery highways on delicate boats that could have been made of glass. Music filled their towns, sad and serious, yet uplifting and beautiful as well, echoing softly over the stark red deserts as well as into deep space. If these people—I preferred to think of them as the real Martians—were aware of the hellish dimension around them, they gave no sign of it. Peter seemed to read my mind.

"I wonder if writers on Earth somehow tuned into these two races and wrote about them," he said. "Mars is often described in literature as both evil and magical."

"It's possible," I replied, thinking that when I returned to Earth as a Wanderer I wanted to write about Mars, preferably about the beautiful race.

We took off for Venus next, and even approaching the second planet from the Sun, we were thrilled by the light and joy that emanated from that white globe. We had to stop far off in space to observe it, the vibrations were so high our ghost bodies couldn't stand it. Through the radiance I glimpsed—and it was only a glimpse—a race of beings much farther along the path of evolution than either humanity or the lovely Martians. It was as if Venus were inhabited by angels, and I understood why on Earth it was usually referred to as the planet of love.

"I don't think we can get any closer," I said.

"We're probably too gross for them," Peter agreed. "I wonder why they are so much ahead of us?"

"I don't know if it's so much a thing of being ahead or behind," I said, once more feeling for the truth inside, something I had begun to do out of habit since talking to the Rishi. I wondered if he had rekindled the ability in me, and if it would follow me back to Earth as a Wanderer. "I think they started before us. They are as we will be in the future."

Peter laughed. "In ten millions years?"

"Maybe it won't take so long," I said, once more feeling I had spoken the truth. The Rishi mentioned a transitional time on Earth, in the next few decades. I wondered if we might not join our cousins on Venus sooner, ghosts included.

Without consciously deciding on our next destination, we began to drift away from Venus and the Sun.

Soon we were out among the globular clusters and nebula. Never in my wildest imagination as a mortal had I imagined such colors, such beauty and vastness of scale. It was as if all my life I had lived in a great palace, but kept my head in the closet. On Earth all I had cared about was who was looking at me and talking about me, while I lived in a universe of mystery and adventure. I made another vow to myself, to study astronomy when I returned as a Wanderer. I did not merely float through the star fields, I merged with them.

"We're all stars," I told Peter.

"Yes. I was thinking how when my father died when I was ten years old I used to search for him in the sky."

A wave of sorrow swept over me, but it was sweet as well, bittersweet like sour candy. "When you died I looked for you in the sky." I reached out, across the light-years, and took his hand. My love for him then was like the light of the stars that shone all around us, and I knew it would burn for ages. "And now I have found you."

He squeezed my hand. He didn't have to say anything.

We floated for ages, seeing more wonders than any starship log could ever record. Eventually we found ourselves at the center of the galaxy. Here the stars were older, as were the myriad races, and the peace and bliss they radiated were like that from a million Venuses combined. Inside, I understood that these people had learned all that this universe had to offer, and that they were merely waiting for the "rest of us" to catch up so that they could go on, where, I didn't know, another dimension perhaps, another creation surely, where God was as real as the sky, and as easy to touch as water in the sea. In the center of this floated what I believe our astronomers would call a galactic black hole. The light that streamed from both the stars and the worlds swirled around the object in a cosmic whirlpool, disappearing down a shaft that seemed to have no bottom. Fascinated, I moved toward it but Peter stopped me.

"We don't know where it goes," he said, and for the first time since he had told me about the Shadow in the days after my death, there was fear in his voice.

"Nothing can harm us," I said. "I want to go inside."

"If you go inside, you might not get out."

I studied him. Throughout our starry journey he had been as enthralled as I was. But now I sensed not only his fear but the reason for it, something had happened to him while we were still on Earth. Yet I couldn't pinpoint the cause, and what it had to do with the portal to infinity that yawned before us. The black hole drew me like a magnet, and I realized we had not stumbled upon it by chance. I had to go in it before I could return to Earth and accomplish my mission.

"I am going," I said. "You can follow me if you wish."

He hesitated. "I'll wait for you, Shari. Take care."

"I am taken care of," I said.

I moved toward the portal.

As stars vanished behind me, so did the *I* that was Shari Cooper.

Words fail me here. How to describe the knowledge of anything without the presence of a knower? In the interior of the black hole the knowledge and the knower were one. I ceased to be aware of things. I was awareness itself.

Still, here, outside of all places, I sensed my true place and finally understood the Rishi's words.

"Our relationship is a beautiful thing. We are, ultimately, the same person, the same being. But if that is too abstract a concept for you, then think of a huge oversoul made up of many souls. Throughout many lives on many worlds, these different souls learn and grow . . ."

I was not singular. Many people were I, and yet we were one as well. All that they had experienced, I had experienced. The different lives the Rishi had spoken of, I had lived them all. I was the Master in Egypt instructing the young student outside in the pyramid. The student was also me. I was enlightened and ignorant at the same time, and I saw it was not possible to have one without the other. No light without darkness. No day without night. No compassion without suffering. No good without evil. Everything worked together, ultimately—a weave of different-colored threads forming an unfathomably rich tapestry. How foolish we were to try to explain the mystery of life, I thought. The mystery could be lived but never explained. Any more than the mind of God could be explained. I felt so close to God right then I imagined myself a perfect fool. And I was happy.

I sensed something else as well. Peter was part of me, as much as the Rishi. It was right that he should be with me enjoying this glimpse of our higher selves. But he was not with me because he was still supposed to be on Earth. He had committed suicide, I remembered that now, and I could see the effect that act had set in motion throughout our oversoul, like a ripple set out across a mountain lake that was finally settling down to freeze for the winter. He had feared to follow me because his fear still followed him. Even this far into eternity. It was this realization that jerked me back into normal space time. Normal as far as ghosts were concerned. I materialized outside the black hole beside Peter.

"What happened?" he asked.

"How long have I been gone?"

"Just an instant."

"It felt like ages." Looking at him I remembered his comment about how the situation on Earth was no longer our concern. I had not discussed what the Rishi told me about my going back as a Wanderer. Now I realized it was because his destiny was separate from mine. I could have fun with him for now, but the fun would have to end.

"What's the matter?" he asked.

"Nothing."

"What happened to you in there?" There was an edge to his voice.

"It's difficult to explain." I reached over and took his hand again. "We have to go back. I have to speak to the Rishi."

"Why?"

Would I miss him on Earth? I asked myself. I missed him now and I hadn't even left him. And he was a part of me. It was such a paradox. How could I succeed as a Wanderer without the love of Peter beside me?

"Because I need his help," I said.

CHAPTER

IX

*J*EAN RODRIGUES drove with Carol Dazmin toward the cemetery where Debra Zimmerer was buried. It was late August; over two months had elapsed since Jean's fall off Lenny Mandez's balcony. The summer had been warm even by Los Angeles standards. Jean had spent the weeks working at her Subway Sandwich job as well as doing volunteer work at the hospital. She had also tried to raise her basic skills in math and science to enter junior college. She was to be tested the next week to see if she could avoid being placed in idiot classes. While she was in high school she had never considered going to college, but now it seemed inevitable that she should go. She was presently trying to talk Carol into joining her.

"I'm not saying a college degree guarantees happiness," Jean said. "But not having one guarantees that you'll be working grunge jobs the rest of your life."

"I don't know," Carol said. "I could become a hairdresser. They make pretty *mucha lana.*"

"You can't spend the rest of your life cutting hair. You'd go mad from boredom."

"But how can I go to college? I'm too stupid. I was hardly able to graduate from high school."

"You're not stupid. You're just lazy. You need to focus. If you could be anything you wanted, what would you choose?"

Carol thought a moment as she steered them down the freeway off-ramp. Debra had been buried across the town from them, at Rose Hills in uptown Whittier. "I'd like to be a rock 'n' roll star."

"You can't go to college to study to be a rock 'n' roll star. Pick something else."

"But that's what I want to do."

"But you can't sing. You can't play an instrument. You can't even dance."

"That's what I'm saying. That's why I should be a hairdresser."

Jean sighed. "You don't have just two choices in life. You have a million. Why don't you study to be a nurse? I think you'd make a great one."

"Would I have to give people shots? Sporty once asked me to shoot him up with heroin and I couldn't do it. I told him to find his own goddamn vein."

"Giving someone a shot that's good for him is a lot different from shooting someone up with heroin. Which reminds me. I heard through the grapevine that Darlene was looking to buy a piece."

Carol nodded. "I heard she's shopping."

"If you heard, then everybody's heard. Surely she can't be planning to go after Juan after all this time."

"I don't know. The timing makes sense to me."

"What do you mean?" Jean asked, although she knew the answer.

Carol shrugged. "Lenny just got out of rehab. He's in a chair. He's mobile. Maybe she's buying the piece for him. Maybe he still wants Juan." Carol added gently, "Maybe he figures he doesn't have much to lose trying for him."

"Damn you! You have to give yourself time. If you can't think of a reason to live, then you have to find one. Think, Lenny, of everything and everyone in the world. Think of something you want to do. Hold on to that, at least until you get out of here."

Jean had not seen Lenny since they had transferred him from the hospital to the rehab clinic in the valley. He had not wanted to see her, which killed her. But she heard from friends that he was looking a lot better, and that gave her some comfort. It was her hope that now that he could get around, he'd call her. She waited for that call.

"He has everything to lose," Jean whispered.

Carol glanced over, concerned. "You're not going to want to hear this, but I'm going to say it anyway. You should start dating other guys."

"You sound like my *mamá.*"

"You should listen to your mother. You love the guy, sure, I love him, too. But his body's wrecked. His life's wrecked. You can't fix it pining away for him."

"His life is not wrecked! He can do everything any other guy can do except walk. That's it. Who needs to walk nowadays? We have cars."

"Can he have sex?"

"I don't know if he can have sex. Many crippled

113

people can. Many crippled people can't. It just depends. And who cares? Despite what all these stupid magazines say, sex isn't everything." Jean was suddenly close to crying. "I can't walk away from him. He needs me. And I need him. You're my best friend. Can't you understand that?"

Carol spoke carefully. "But he doesn't even call you, Jean."

Jean nodded. "He will. When he's feeling better, he'll call. I know it."

Carol stopped at a light and stared at her. "You're still so different from when we were growing up. Before your fall, you would have been out with another guy while Lenny was still in surgery."

Jean forced a smile. "I wasn't that bad."

"You were no saint." Carol sighed. "I'm sorry I said what I did. If you want to go on loving Lenny, more power to you. Look at me, I can't even make up my mind whether I want to sleep with guys or girls."

"Are you still seeing Scarface?"

"No. But I go out with his sister every now and then." She nodded at the manila envelope Jean carried. "Is that your story for Debra?"

"Yes. It was the first story I ever thought up. I told her the beginning, but I only figured out how it should end last week. I hope she likes it." Jean laughed at her own foolishness, and also got a little teary. "I know she's not there in that hole in the ground where they put her body. But I want to read it to her at her grave because I think maybe she'll know I'm there somehow. Does that make sense?"

"It does to me." Carol paused. "Maybe I should become a mortician."

"Just keep driving."

"Can I read the story after you've read it to Debra?"

"Seguro."

"Are you going to try to get it published?"

"I hadn't really thought about that. But the main character is a successful author. I wonder if I subconsciously patterned her after myself." Jean added, wiping at her eyes, "I see myself being like her some day."

"Have you been working on other stories?"

"Yes. Late at night. I write in a spiral notebook with a Flair pen."

Carol cast her another look. "You never did that before your fall."

Jean nodded thoughtfully. "I know."

She never got headaches before her fall, either. They had become less frequent, but had never left completely. Sometimes she wondered if she had hurt herself worse than the doctors knew. She tried not to think about it.

Rose Hills was lovely. Many acres of well-tended lawns weaving in and around the Whittier Hills. Jean had attended Debra's funeral and still kept in loose contact with her father. Jean directed Carol toward a shaded meadow. Carol offered to stay in the car without being asked, and for that Jean was grateful. Jean had brought Debra a handful of flowers as well as her story. Jean laid the daisies beside the simple metal marker that was all that was left to say Debra had come and gone. Yet Jean felt her friend close as she lifted up the handful of pages to read aloud.

"Debra, I've reworked this three times and I don't know if I can make it any better," she said. "It's either completely brilliant or totally stupid. But it's my first story and I'm proud of it. If I ever do get it published, I'll be sure to dedicate it to you. Please forgive the crude spots ahead of time. What can I say? I have a dirty mind." She cleared her throat. "The story, as you might remember, is entitled, 'Where Do You Get Your Ideas?' If you get bored fly back to heaven. I won't hold it against you."

Debra Zimmerer was working on her latest novel when the creature came out of her bedroom closet. She almost fell off her chair when she saw the thing. She rubbed her eyes, hoping he'd go away, but he didn't. He was ugly, short, and dark as a dwarf from a deep cave, scaly and smelly as a troll from beneath an ancient bridge. Clearly, he was not human. As he walked toward her desk she couldn't help but notice his big yellow teeth and wide green eyes. He didn't smell especially pleasant, either. She had no idea what he'd been doing in her closet.

"Hi, Debbie," he said. "What's happening?"

Debra took an immediate dislike to him. She let no one call her Debbie. She was either Debra or Melissa Monroe, the pen name she wrote under, or else simply Ms. M & M. She had a few names because she was one of America's best-selling authors, and she felt it only fitting that someone as popular as she should be able to slip in and out of several identities. Just before the troll had come out of her closet, she had been typing hard on her new novel, *The Color of Pain*. She had a tight deadline, and as always was late. Indeed, she had been up most of the previous night working on the last chapters and was exhausted. She wondered if her fatigue had something to do with her seeing the troll. Her novel was in the horror genre, but otherwise it had nothing to do with the creature standing beside her desk.

"Who the hell are you?" she asked.

He smiled, and as he did so gray-colored slobber leaked out the sides of his wide toothy mouth. His nose was thick, the nostrils pointing almost straight out, choked with white hairs. He wore a baggy pair of black shorts, snakeskin slippers, no shirt. The muscles on his hairy green chest were knotted and hard. Even though he was only three feet tall, he looked strong, perhaps stronger than she was, she didn't know.

"My name's Sam," he said. "I'm your muse."

Debra reached over and turned off her computer screen. "Come again?"

"I'm your muse. You know, the one who gives you your ideas. You get asked that question all the time—where do you get your ideas? Well, now you know. You're looking at him."

Debra shook her head. "That's ridiculous. Muses are supposed to be beautiful angels. You look like something the dog dug up."

He lost his smile. "Careful, Debbie. I don't like cracks about my looks. And if you think you have an angel for a muse, then you better think again. Look at the kind of stories you write. They're filled with ghouls and vampires and psychos. Somebody's always getting murdered in them. What do you think—an angel would give you those stories? Get a clue, sister. You want to write horror—you get a muse like me. It's that simple."

Debra frowned. "What is your name?"

"Sam. Sam O'Connor."

"Are you Irish?" He had a trace of the accent.

"On my mother's side. But I'm no leprechaun, if that's what you're thinking."

"What were you doing in my closet?"

"That's where I live. I have to stay close or you wouldn't be able to write nothing."

"You used a double negative. What you mean to say is, I wouldn't be able to write anything. That's pretty basic grammar. You should know that if you're really my muse."

Sam waved his hand. "I don't care about all that crap. Grammar is for editors and pansies. I'm the one who gives the blood and guts to your stories. If it wasn't for me, you would be writing about teen problems and teacher-student conflicts. You wouldn't be selling anything and you'd be living in a dump." He reached out to turn her monitor back on. "You sure as hell wouldn't be writing a book as clever as *The Color of Pain*. Let me see that last chapter. I think I can tell you how it should end."

She slapped his hand away. "Don't you dare look at my work. I don't let anyone see it till it's done."

Sam stared at his hand as if she had stabbed a knife in rather than knocked it aside. His face darkened; his teeth seemed to lengthen; the pupils of his eyes narrowed to hard green slits. He took a step back and glared up at her.

"Let's get one thing straight from the start," he said. "It's not *your* work, it's *our* work. And if you want our work to continue, you're going to have to learn to play by a few new rules. Understand, Debbie?"

"Don't call me that. No one calls me that."

"Liar. When you were in school all your friends called you that. But now that you think you're such a big shot, you go by Debra or that other stupid name you put on our books. But you're no big shot to me. You're nothing without me."

Debra gave a smug chuckle. "You keep saying that, but this house and everything in it belongs to me. I bought it with the money I made selling thirty million books. How many books have you sold? None, I bet. You look like a loser to me, Sam O'Connor. You look like a—something despicable."

Sam smiled grimly. "You were about to call me a colorful simile, but you couldn't think of one, could you? You can't think of anything clever without me. Go ahead, try, I dare you. I look like a what?"

Debra thought for a moment, but nothing special came to her. "You look like one ugly bastard," she said finally.

He laughed. "That's it? That's the best you can come up with? How many books are you going to sell describing your villains as 'one ugly bastard'? And what are you going to say about your heroes? Oh, they were so handsome? So pretty? You're going to be searching your thesaurus soon, Debbie, if you don't cooperate. And you'll find it can't help you with your plot." Again, he reached for her monitor button. "Let me see how you're wrecking my story."

She didn't stop him as he turned on the screen, but said, "How can you say it's your story when I thought it up, in my own head?"

Sam studied her last page. "All us muses are sort of telepathic. The story may have ended in your head, but only because I put it there in the first place." He grunted at the screen. "You can't kill Alisa here. You need her for the sequel."

"What sequel? There's no sequel to this book. Alisa's going to die and that's the end of it. Finished."

"You see what I mean? You don't even know that this first book is the beginning of a trilogy. The second and third books are going to be better than the first. You can't kill the girl. If you do you'll be out a million dollars in royalties."

Debra felt exasperated. Of course, when she thought about it, she remembered she had felt that way *before* Sam appeared. "How come I didn't know that?" she asked.

"Because I didn't tell you," Sam said. "I waited to tell you until after I came out of the closet. I knew it would make you more open to my proposition."

"What proposition is that?"

Sam's smile returned. He glanced around her well-furnished spacious bedroom, then out the window at the forest and the ocean. "You got it pretty good here, girl. You live in a mansion. You drive a hot car. You have a maid to clean up your messes and a secretary to take care of your bills and correspondence. You don't have to do anything except write."

"But writing's hard work. I deserve my success."

Sam snorted. "Writing's hard work when your muse goes on vacation. But how hard do you really work? You can sit down and knock out a novel in a month. That's because you got me working for you in the closet. I do all the heavy thinking. You're just a glorified typist. Sometimes I'm up till two or three in the morning trying to figure out a plot line, and then you get to wake up fresh in the morning and there it is all ready for you. I'm sick of this arrangement. I'm tired of the closet. I want to enjoy more of the fruits of my creativity. From now on, Debbie, you're going to give me a piece of the action."

Debra sat back and crossed her arms over her chest. "How big a piece?"

"For starters, fifty percent of everything you make."

Debra laughed. "Gimme a break. I make millions a year. You think I'm just going to hand over half of that to you? You get a clue, brother."

Sam lost his smile. "Fine. You want to play hard ball, let's see how hard your head is." He pointed to the screen. "Finish this book right now. Write the last page."

"I can't write with a slimy troll like you standing beside me."

Sam put his scaly hand on her knee. He pinched her leg, ever so slightly, and chewed on his tongue as if wishing it were one of her fingers. "I told you, no cracks about my appearance. If you spent as much time as I have in a closet, you wouldn't look any better. But as a favor to you, and to prove my point, I am willing to wait in the other room while you write the last page. You come get me when you're done. Or more likely, you come get me when you realize you have nothing in your brain to write about." He released his grip and patted her knee gently. He even smiled again, although his eyes remained cold. "You take as long as you want, Debbie."

Debra wiped the spot where he had touched her. "The name's Debra."

Sam walked toward the door, calling over his shoulder. "The *names* will be Sam O'Connor and Melissa

Monroe. From now on, that's what'll appear on your books, in that order. That's another of my conditions."

Debra wanted to spit at him. "Never."

Sam laughed as he left. "Never say never."

He was gone two seconds when Debra turned back to her word processor and began to type furiously. His challenge was a piece of cake, she thought. What was one more page out of three hundred? She just had to have her heroine—well, all right, maybe she shouldn't kill her. Alisa was a great character and there were at least another two books in her. Debra could see that now. Sam was right. But she could finish with Alisa for now without his advice. She just had to have the girl—what? How could she save her? She had it all set up to kill her. Maybe she could— Maybe if she just— No, that wouldn't work. That would be stupid, and if she had a stupid ending, that's all people would remember. Three hundred pages of brilliant prose, and people would throw it against the wall and tell their friends not to buy it if the last page was flubbed. She always prided herself on her fantastic last pages. OK, she thought, stay cool and do what you do best. You know you're better than the rest, Ms. M & M, Ms. *New York Times* Best-Selling Author. *Just write the goddamn page!*

Two hours later Debra went out to see Sam. He was sitting in her favorite chair with his ugly feet up on the coffee table eating the turkey sandwich she had planned to have for lunch. He had the TV turned to the sci-fi channel, some old black-and-white monster flick. He laughed uproariously as the alien monster ate a cute, well-proportioned brunette who bore a vague resemblance to her. He barely looked up as she entered.

"All right," she said bitterly. "How does the stupid book end?"

He glanced over and took another big bite out of her sandwich. "It ends in a cliff hanger," he said. "The reader doesn't know whether Alisa makes it or not."

"That's it? That's no ending."

"You're wrong. It's the perfect ending. But how you do it is important. I'll fix it up after my show." He paused and nodded to the nearby couch. "I want to go over a few more of my conditions. Just so we understand each other."

Feeling miserable, she sat down. He was right about the ending, she realized. He must have been helping her with her books since the days of *Slumber Weekend,* the first book she ever sold. Before then she had written plots like a—damn, she couldn't describe to herself how poorly she had plotted. Hell, and he knew it, too—he was snickering at her again.

"Besides wanting half your income and my name on every book," he began, "my picture is to appear on the back flap beside yours. We'll hire a professional photographer who can touch up my rough edges, give me a yuppie look. Also, we're firing your agent. He gets ten percent and he does nothing. From now on I'll negotiate all our contracts. I'll get us bigger advances, higher royalties. And I want to take over your fan mail. There are a lot of cute babes who write you. I want to get to know them, and let them get to know me. I want them to know just who turns them on in the middle of the night. And give me your car keys. I have a date tonight."

"But I just bought that car," she protested. "It's the only one I have."

Sam chuckled. "Then I guess you'll be staying home tonight. Maybe you can brush up on your grammar. It's all you're good for, Debbie." He took another bite from his sandwich and let out a loud belch. "You might as well face it—I'm the talent."

Debra had a horrible time firing her agent. He had been with her from the start. He pleaded with her to reconsider, begged her to tell him whom she had found to take his place. Finally, when she told him nothing, he threatened to sue her. She hung up. She had received a legal-looking letter from him a few days earlier but was afraid to open it. Sam told her not to worry. He said he knew a great lawyer. He seemed to know a lot of people for having spent so much time in her closet.

She had invited a photographer out to shoot Sam, but the guy had fled the moment he saw her muse, which put Sam in a bad mood. He continued to be sensitive about his appearance. She had ended up photographing him herself and had an expert rework the negatives. The expert kept asking her what the joke was. It didn't seem Sam would ever look like a yuppie.

Sam had taken over her bedroom. She now lived in one of the smaller rooms at the front of the house with no view. She had purchased another car, but Sam had put a ceiling on how much she could spend. She had ended up replacing her new Mercedes with a used Ford. Sam laughed at her every time she went out to start it.

He had *no* dates, however, even though he said he did. He went out often but returned fast, and usually in a lousy mood. He scoured her fan mail for eligible young women. She heard him flirting with them on the phone, setting up lunches and dinners. She could just imagine the women's reactions when they finally met the genius behind the books they loved. She had suggested he join a dating club, but he had told her to shut up.

They had started immediately on a new book, a horror story for teens. Debra had written Young Adult novels for several years before breaking into main-stream fiction, and still enjoyed the form. She'd wanted to take a break after completing her—*their*—adult novel, but Sam had insisted she keep writing. Yet his input from outside the closet was not as easy to take as it had been from inside. He paced ceaselessly behind her as she worked, muttering swear words and personal insults as often as he did fresh lines of dialogue.

"All right," he said when they got stuck in the middle of a particularly violent scene. "We can't pull any punches here. We've got to go for visceral impact. Write, 'Maria shot Tom directly in the belly. The blast went right through his guts and painted the wall behind him a lumpy red. Tom stared at Maria and tried to speak. A portion of his lower intestines and pieces of yesterday's lunch dripped out the side of his mouth. His breath stunk like an outhouse. Cursing

Maria and her mother to eternal damnation, he slumped to the floor. A stunned silence choked the room.'" Sam paused and grunted in satisfaction. "Write that, Debbie, word for word."

"Wait a second," Debra said. "Are we forgetting something here? This is a Young Adult book. We don't have lower intestines and yesterday's lunch dripping out the side of people's mouths. Our editor won't stand for it. Neither will the teachers and librarians. We have to tone it down."

Sam was suddenly enraged. "I never tone down my words! What I have just told you is perfect. You write it that way or you stop writing altogether."

That was a typical retort from Sam. If she didn't do what he said, she could hang up her career. What he didn't seem to realize was how close she was to saying, "Fine. Take the money and the Mercedes. I can get another job. Just get out of my house and stop sleazing all over my fans." But she had books left on her contract to finish, this Young Adult novel being one of them. She feared getting stuck with half a dozen lawsuits and no income coming in. Plus she doubted there was anything else she could do, except maybe be a full-time secretary for some sexist male executive. She cautioned herself to speak carefully before responding.

"I have written dozens of Young Adult books," she said. "If what you say is true, I have written them with your help. Together we have pushed the limits of the genre. But there are certain limits it would be a mistake to go beyond. We can shoot Tom in the guts, and we can even talk about the blood that gushes out. But that's as graphic as we can get. There are even more rules when it comes to sex. None of our characters can have sex onstage."

"What do you mean onstage?" Sam growled.

"None of our characters are in the school drama club. They can do it in their cars or at the park. Which reminds me. I have a great scene planned for the middle of the book. After Carol and Larry have been turned into aliens, and been killed by the police, we'll have them rise from the dead and make love in the morgue with formaldehyde dripping all over each other from their gory wounds. That will give us another half million in sales, I guarantee it."

Debra leaned over and turned off the computer. "If we write that scene we guarantee ourselves zero sales."

"No way!"

"Yes, way! The publisher won't accept the book."

"Then we'll get another publisher. New York City is riddled with them. I don't know why you stay with that house you're at. Most of what they publish is written by failed actresses and politicians trying to lose weight."

"It's not that simple. The same rules will apply wherever we go."

"Rules?" Sam said indignantly. "I'm an artist. I don't have to follow rules. Do you think J.R.R. Tolkien was worried about rules when we wrote *The Lord of the Rings?*"

Debra paused. "Are you insinuating that you were Tolkien's muse?"

"Damn right I was. Where do you think he got the Ents and the Orcs? I made those up, not him."

"Well, I can see you and the Orcs," Debra mumbled.

Sam took a step closer. "I didn't quite catch that?"

Debra cleared her throat. "We're going to have to argue about this later. I have to meet my younger sister, Ann, for lunch."

Sam stopped and smiled. "Your sister, hey? I've seen Ann's picture in the other room. She's a babe. How about me coming to lunch with you two? You can introduce the two of us, tell her how creative I am." He grinned and winked. "In all kinds of ways."

Debra stood hastily. "You're not meeting my sister."

Sam stepped in front of her as she moved toward the door. "Why not? You don't think I'm good enough for her? How many other guys can she meet that have my imagination?"

"None." Debra shook her head. "That's not my point."

"What is your point? You think she won't find me attractive?"

"You're not exactly her type."

"What is her type?"

"Well."

"Ah! You still think I'm ugly!"

"I didn't say that. It's just that, well, you are kind of short."

"I can wear my platform shoes. I bought some the other day."

"That would help. But it's not the main problem."

"What is the main problem? Is it my face? I can get these scales removed. I'm going to see a plastic surgeon on Thursday. I'll tell Ann I'm recovering from a fire."

"No! You won't tell Ann anything. You're not going to meet her."

Sam paused and nodded to himself. "So that's the way it is." He drew himself up on his hairy toes as he did when he was about to make a threat. "If you don't introduce me to Ann, I don't tell you how this new book ends. I'll let you work on it until the last chapter, and then when your editor's screaming for the manuscript, I'll leave you hanging."

Debra had had enough. She defiantly thrust her hands onto her hips. "Go ahead! Stop helping me! I've made enough money to live on for the rest of my life even if you take half. Go find another writer to play muse to. Get a nerdy teenage boy who looks up cheerleaders' skirts. I'm sure you'll get along fabulously."

Unfortunately, much to her surprise, Sam was not impressed by her retort to his threat. He let out a sly chuckle. "You'll live on half of what, Debbie? I copyrighted the plots of each of your books before you even wrote them. I have certified letters mailed to myself containing detailed outlines of every one of your stories. You walk out on me now, and I'll drag you into court and sue your ass off. The whole world will know that you're nothing but a scam. You'll owe me more money than you have. You'll have to sell that old Ford you're driving just to buy food."

Debra stared at him. "You're bluffing. You ruin me, you ruin yourself."

Sam grinned. "I can always make another you. But where are you going to find another me?"

Debra brushed him aside. "I'm going to lunch with my sister."

Sam let her pass. "That's fine," he called after her. "As long as you tell Ann I'll be calling her for dinner soon. At her place!"

Debra did not enjoy her afternoon meal, even though she ordered her favorite food at her favorite restaurant. She picked at her swordfish and stared out the window at the ocean. Her sister asked her what was bothering her, but she just shrugged and said she was under a lot of pressure because of a deadline. Finally lunch was over and she was able to kiss her sister goodbye and think seriously about what she was up against. Not for a moment did she consider telling Ann about Sam. It made her sick just to think of that smelly creature touching her sister.

She thought seriously but not creatively, and that was the core of her problem. Her enemy was her inspiration. She couldn't destroy him unless he helped her, which was not likely in the next fifty years. What to do? She had to go to someone else for her ideas. But who could she ask? Who would even believe her story?

Then it struck her.

She was a storyteller, still, at least in the eyes of the world, even if, apparently, she couldn't think up an opening line without her troll cackling in the background. But no one knew that yet, she reassured herself. Among other writers, she was seen as brilliant. Why couldn't she go to another writer, present her dilemma as a plot problem, and have him solve it? She knew just the man, Scott Alan. He was a local author of horror stories. He had yet to hit it big, but he had published a number of well-reviewed novels. She had considered him something of a beginner, but secretly she thought he was at least as, if not more so, creative than herself. He would probably be thrilled to help out *The New York Times* Best-Selling Melissa Monroe.

She drove to Scott Alan's house after finding his address in the book.

His face shone excitedly when he answered the door. He invited her in. Wow, it was neat of her to stop by. Could he get her something to drink or eat? He'd loved her last book. How long had it stayed on the *Times* list? Four months? Amazing, he said. She was amazing.

"Thank you," Debra said as she took a seat on his couch. "I loved your last book as well."

He grinned. He was a handsome young man in his late thirties with sandy-colored hair and blue eyes and a nice round face that—damn! She couldn't think what his face was like. But it was attractive enough, she thought. Not that she wanted to have sex with him in a morgue or anything kinky like that. Where did Sam get such disgusting ideas?

"What did you like about it the most?" Scott asked.

Debra hesitated. Actually, she hadn't read his last book. "I liked how the main character changed as the novel progressed."

"Which main character was that?"

She smiled. "You know, Scott, the one who was on the most pages."

Scott was doubtful. "You mean Lucifer, the robot? I guess he did kind of change." Scott chuckled. "When he blew up."

"That's what I mean, yeah, exactly. You blew him

up and his whole perspective changed." Debra paused. "Scott, I'm working on a short story for an anthology of major horror writers and I'm stuck." She batted her long brown lashes, knowing she could look pretty sexy to a struggling author. "I was wondering if you could help me get unstuck?"

He was interested. "What's the problem?"

"It's kind of unusual," she began. "My main character's a famous author and she has this troll for a muse. . . ."

It took Debra almost an hour to tell her story. She hesitated to leave out any detail for fear she might skip over the weak point in Sam's armor. Scott listened intently, as if she were telling him a real-life dilemma, which just happened to be the case. When she was done, he sat thoughtful for a moment.

"This story isn't like any of your others," he said finally.

"Tell me about it," she muttered.

"I'm not saying it's not clever. It's just that it's not as based in reality as most of your work."

"That may be why I'm having trouble resolving the main conflict. But you know what they say, if you don't take chances sometimes, you'll never know— you'll never know . . ."

"You'll never know what?"

Debra blushed. She had been about to make up a saying, but of course she couldn't think of what to say. "Never mind. Can you help me? How can my character get rid of her muse?"

"Does she still want to keep him as her muse? Or just put him back in the closet?"

Debra shook her head miserably. "At this point I think she'd be happy just to have him out of her life."

"How strong is this troll?"

"Pretty strong. Stronger than she is. Why do you ask?"

"For the obvious reason. Why can't she just buy a gun and kill him?"

"Believe me, she's thought of it."

"And?"

"She's not a killer—she's a writer, remember?" Debra added, "But if she were sure she could pull it off, and not get hurt, she might consider it."

"But the preferable ending would be to get the troll back in the closet and once more help your main character write her stories?"

"Yes."

"You mentioned that the troll said he was telepathic. Can he read the woman's mind?"

Debra had considered that point. For the most part, except when they were working together, Sam seemed unable to tune in to her thoughts. For example, the day before she had decided to cook them both vegetarian lasagna for dinner. But he had exploded when she served him the food. He needed meat, he yelled, didn't she know better?

"He's sensitive to the woman's thoughts," she said carefully. "But I don't know if he can read them, at least not all the time."

"But it would be better to distract him just before striking the decisive blow?"

"Yes. Definitely. But how is she supposed to distract a troll?"

Scott smiled. "I'm surprised it hasn't occurred to you, Debra. His weak spot is obvious. He's intelligent but insecure in his relationships with women. He worries he's unattractive. What we need your main character to do is pretend to seduce him, and then just when they're about to go to bed, she can ask him to get contraceptives from the closet. He'll be so excited he'll do anything she wants. The moment he steps inside, she can slam the door shut and lock him in."

Debra was appalled. "But she can't pretend to seduce him. Just being around him makes her nauseated."

"But she has to pretend. She has no choice."

"What makes you think he's interested in her?"

"Is she attractive?"

Debra brushed her hair with her hand. "Well, yes. She's pretty cute, I think."

"Then he'll be interested. It sounds like they have a love-hate relationship as it is."

Debra was shocked. "She can't stand to be in the same room with him. How can you say she loves him?"

Scott waved her objection away. "That's also obvious. The way they carry on together. There's got to be some attraction there, on both sides."

"No way."

"It doesn't matter. She just has to get him in the closet and lock the door. Now, if she wants to keep him as her muse, she has to give him some incentive while he's there. Perhaps she should have a phone installed in her closet. Then if he keeps helping her write, she can tell him, she'll keep slipping fresh fan letters under his door and pay for his AT&T bill."

Debra brightened. "That's interesting. He loves talking on the phone. It's practically his only pleasure in life, besides eating." She nodded. "You're pretty good."

"Thank you. You're not too bad yourself."

"Yeah." She glanced down the hall toward his bedroom, feeling a sudden chill from that direction. "Scott?"

"What?"

"Where do you get your ideas?"

He laughed. "You must get asked that question all the time. You know the answer as well as I do. I don't know. They just come to me." He paused. "What's the matter?"

She tried to hear if there was any other sound in the house. A pair of ugly feet scampering about in a closed space, for example. But there was no one about except the two of them.

"Nothing," she said softly. "I was just wondering."

At first Sam greeted her idea to go to a play with her that evening with suspicion. But when he saw she was serious, he did an about-face and got all excited, and even said a few kind words to her about her writing. It had been part of her plan to suggest he go out and buy himself a new outfit to wear on the date—so that she could have time to prepare the closet—but he beat her to the mark by bringing up the idea of new clothes. He promised to be back by sunset and jumped in her Mercedes and was gone. She immediately got on the phone to a handyman, telling him it was an emergency. He said he'd be right over.

Debra wanted two modifications made to the closet. Besides having a separate phone line installed, she instructed the man to add a sturdy dead bolt to the door. Once she had Sam inside, she swore to herself, she was not letting him out. The handyman worked quickly and was in and out in less than an hour.

She made a reservation for the play and dressed with care for their date. The trouble was, she didn't know what turned a troll on. She had to think back to what the naughty girls in her books wore to get a guy's attention and realized that probably with Sam, less was more. She put on a mini skirt from her high school days and let her thick brown hair hang down her back. Sam was true to his word and was back before sunset. He took one look at her, let out an obscene whistle and hurried off to one of the bathrooms with his collection of Nordstrom bags. She managed to keep him away from the master bedroom with the excuse that she needed to use it just this once because the lighting was better to finish her makeup. He was in such a good mood he didn't argue with her.

She had said a play and not added dinner because she didn't want to be seen with him too much since she did have to live in the town. But Sam insisted they get a bite to eat before going to the theater. He took her to a French restaurant downtown. He had on a dark gray suit and a white shirt with a very chic green silk tie. She didn't know how he'd had them fit to his size. He wore oversize sunglasses to hide as much of his face as possible, and was somewhat successful with the maneuver. The maître d' acted as if she was with a dwarf who'd just had skin grafts.

"To a long and successful partnership," Sam toasted when the wine arrived. He raised his glass and added with a wink that was visible even through his sunglasses, "To a deeply satisfying relationship. Cheers."

She smiled and raised her glass and tried not to vomit. "Cheers."

He took a sip of his wine and set his glass down and touched her right knee underneath the table. "You look lovely tonight, my dear. What is that perfume you're wearing?"

"Ecstasy."

Sam was in heaven. "My favorite. How did you know?"

"It's sensual. You're sensual." She blushed. "I just thought the two would go together."

He continued to stroke her leg, but he studied her as well. "What brought about the sudden interest, Deb —Debra?"

She shrugged. "I don't know. I guess it was spending time with you and seeing how brilliant you are. Nothing turns me on as much as intelligence." She paused, wanting to get a grip on just how much he could read her mind. "You should know that about me."

He grinned. "Opposites attract."

She nodded. "Ain't that the truth."

"Ain't? Isn't that poor grammar?"

She clasped his hand under the table and gave it a warm squeeze. "Tonight, for once, let's forget grammar. Let's use all the naughty words we want."

Sam licked his chops. "Jesus," he said.

Their meals came. Debra had halibut, Sam steak, a thick cut as rare as the health department allowed. Briefly she wondered how he had survived in her closet for so many years without food but assumed eating was a pleasure with him and not a necessity. She wouldn't be feeding him once she had him locked away.

The play turned out to be a nightmare. They sat in the back in the dark, and Sam couldn't keep his hands off her. Her pushing him away seemed to get him more aroused. She took in so little of the storyline that she couldn't have said what it was about. Her nerves were frayed. What if he escaped? What manner of revenge would he take? She thought of all the tortures the villains in her books had inflicted on her characters. All inspired by Sam. She could not fail, it was as simple as that.

He started to kiss her the moment they returned home. Or tried to—he was too short to do more than stick his face in her bosom and slobber on her blouse. He had brushed his teeth and gargled but his breath still stank. He dragged her toward the bedroom. With bile rising in her throat, she went with him.

He wanted her to undress in front of him with the lights on.

"Do it slowly," he said, his big yellow teeth chattering with excitement. "Not like they do it in teenage books. Like *you're* onstage."

She forced a smile. "Shouldn't we lower the lights? It's so much more romantic." She didn't want him getting too good a look at the closet when she steered him in that direction. He shook his head.

"I want to see you, Debra. See what you've got. I've waited a long time for this, you know."

She kicked off her shoes and began to unbutton her blouse. "Have you now? But *you* must know, Sam, that you can't tell what a girl's got until you've got your hands on her. And then it's so much better without all this artificial illumination." Sighing with pleasure, she removed her top and let it drop to the floor. Sam's big green eyes bugged out of his head. She crooned, "Something about the dark really turns me on."

"I'll get the lights," Sam panted. He tried turning off the lamp but his hands were shaking so badly he ended up having to yank the plug out of the wall to kill the light. The room was plunged into darkness. She could still see him, though, his phosphorescent eyes moving toward her. "Love me, baby," he whispered as his stubby arms went around her waist. He tried to press her down onto the bed. She stroked the top of his head and leaned over and spoke in his ear.

"You've got me so hot, Sam. I want to do it with you again and again. But I can't get pregnant. You understand. A baby would spoil everything we've got going here. You've got to wear something."

Sam's voice came out disappointed. "But I didn't buy anything."

She giggled mischievously. "Don't worry. I've got something in the closet, on the bottom shelf. You go get it and I'll help you put it on."

He let go of her and slapped her on her butt with pleasure. "That's my girl! Always thinking of the details. I'll get it and just pray it fits. Let me tell you, Debra, you haven't had a man until you've had your muse."

"Hurry," she whispered at him. Her eyes had adjusted to the dark somewhat, and she could see his short squat outline as he walked to the closet and poked his head inside. She took a step toward his back, but just then his glowing green eyes turned her way. She froze.

"I don't see them," he said. "Maybe I should turn the light back on."

"They're in the corner," she said quickly. "Keep looking. Please don't turn on the light. It will spoil the mood."

"Not for me." He snickered, turning back to the closet. "I'm always in the mood."

"So am I," Debra muttered. Suddenly she was sick of the charade, of having to constantly kiss his ass. She had planned to wait until she had talked him all the way into the closet before she struck, but now she couldn't wait a second longer. In two long strides she moved up behind him. He heard her approach; once more his green eyes turned in her direction as she raised her bare right foot and planted it firmly on his mid back. But even at that late a moment, he didn't realize his peril.

"Oh," he moaned with delight. "That feels good. Do it harder."

"My pleasure." She gave him one hard shove and he toppled forward into the closet. He might have hit his head on the far wall, she wasn't sure. She heard a loud bump followed by a soft thud. In a flash she grabbed hold of the door and slammed it shut, twisting the bolt counterclockwise as the handyman had instructed her. Hardly had she set the lock in place than he began to bang on the door.

"Debra!" he shouted. "Let me out!"

She laughed. "You didn't say please, Sam. If you

had said please, I might have considered it. But now it's too late."

He threw his whole body against the door, but it was sturdy and didn't budge an inch. "If you don't let me out right now, it'll be the end of Melissa Monroe. There'll be no more warped teenagers. No more alien vampires. You'll be writing self-help and diet books for the rest of your life. You'll have to do talk shows to sell copies."

Debra couldn't stop laughing. "You say that now, Sam, but you're going to get pretty bored in there with nothing to do. Especially after your taste of freedom. I know you—you love your horror. Soon enough you'll be giving me stories again."

"Never!"

"Never say never."

He continued to pound on the door. "Let me out, you bitch!"

"What did you call me Sam? The *B* word? Golly, I don't know if that's allowed. I'll have to check with my editor and get back to you. We might have to cross that out."

"Debra!"

"That's my name. Be sure you don't forget it. Oh, by the way, I had a phone installed in the closet this afternoon. If you behave yourself and continue to help me on my stories, I might slip you a letter from a hot fan to call every now and then."

He stopped pounding. "Can I call long distance?" he asked.

"Only if our latest book makes *The New York Times* list."

Sam considered. "Can't I come out on weekends?"

"No way. I'll never get you back in the closet."

He sounded kind of sad. "Was all of tonight just a sham to lock me up?"

"I'm afraid so, Sam. You're just not my type."

He was curious. "Where did you get the idea to do this?"

Debra grinned in the dark. "I'll let you figure that one out."

A week later Debra stopped by Scott's house to thank him for help with *her story*. She was surprised when a short mole of a woman with a wide hat and thick sunglasses answered the door. Because the woman stood in the shadows, and it was bright and sunny outside, Debra couldn't get a good look at her. But she could have sworn the woman had *purple* hair.

"Can I help you?" the woman asked in a deep sober voice. She sounded like a cannibal might after a late-night dinner—the simile just popped into Debra's mind. Her thick red coat covered most of her squat figure. She wore black satin gloves and kept her right hand on the edge of the door.

"Yes," Debra said. "I'm here to see Scott. Is he at home?"

"Scott doesn't live here anymore." The woman started to shut the door. "Have a nice day."

Debra shot out her arm. "Wait a second. What do you mean he doesn't live here? I visited him here last week. Who are you?"

The woman stared up at her with her dark glasses. There was something wrong with her skin. It looked burnt, peeling, while at the same time it was ashen.

Debra couldn't help noticing how large her hands were, bigger than Sam's for that matter.

"A relative," the woman said.

"Where has Scott moved to? Do you have a forwarding address?"

"No."

"Do you know why he left so suddenly?"

"No."

Debra frowned. "If you see him would you tell him Melissa Monroe stopped by."

"The writer?"

"Yes, that's me."

The woman seemed to grin. Yet the expression was hard to classify as a simple smile because there was gloating in it. As if the woman were still hungry after her late snack and wanted dessert. Her tone took on a false note of sweetness.

"I love writers," she said. "Would you like to come in, dear? Maybe for some tea? We could discuss books."

Debra swallowed and took a step back, feeling a strong sense of déjà vu. "No thank you. I have an appointment in half an hour. I really must run. But please, remember to give Scott my message."

The woman nodded. "It will be my pleasure."

"Thank you," Debra said. As she turned toward her car, just before the woman closed the front door, she thought she heard someone pounding on a wall somewhere deep in the house. She paused to listen closer, but just then the woman shut the door and she heard nothing more, not even the woman moving inside.

"Must have been my imagination," she muttered to herself.

Yet as Debra Zimmerer, *New York Times* Best-Selling Author, started her car and pulled out of the driveway, she wondered if she wanted to stay in the writing business, even if Sam continued to help her. She had the feeling that being a horror author was a lot more dangerous than it was cracked up to be.

Jean laughed out loud as she finished reading her last line. "I like how Scott got put in the closet, too. It appeals to my ghoulish nature. But you know, Debra, it also makes me nervous about where I get *my* ideas." Jean paused to wipe away another tear. Her voice became softer. "But you might know that—wherever you are. If our ideas really do come from angels, then put in a good word for me with them. Have them send me down a story for a best seller. I can't make sandwiches at Subway the rest of my life." She paused and touched the marker. This date to that date, she thought. Eighteen years in between. It didn't seem right that an all-loving God could give a person so little time. She had only known Debra ten days, but she still missed her. Biting her lip, she traced Debra's name with her fingertips. "I will remember you," she whispered.

I want people to remember me.

Jean jerked back from the marker. Who had said that? The voice seemed to come out of the air. Of course, she thought, that was ridiculous. The voice had been in her mind. Just her own thoughts.

Yet the line felt as if it had been spoken by another.

The memory of that bloody stain on the condo concrete came back to her.

"I thought you knew her."
"Knew who?"
"The girl who died here."

Jean thought of James Cooper. After she had helped him move, he had taken her straight home and dropped her off. He had asked for her number, however, but he had not called her. She had been careful not to mention Lenny around him—not out of an urge to cheat on her boyfriend—more out of an innocent desire to get to know James better. Or was her desire so innocent? She did not lust after the guy. Nevertheless, she desperately wanted something from him, something she couldn't explain even to herself. Why hadn't he called her?

Because you spooked him as much as he spooked you.

Yet she had never asked him about his dead sister. Something Cooper.

"I suppose we all want to be remembered," Jean said in a shaky voice to Debra Zimmerer's grave marker. Gathering her story together, leaving the flowers behind, she stood and walked slowly back to the car. Carol snored behind the wheel. Jean woke her and said, "Take me home."

Yes, she thought, she wanted to go home. But first she had to find it.

Jean found James Cooper's phone number without difficulty. Information had it. But calling him proved to be more difficult. Alone in her bedroom, she dialed the number a half dozen times but quickly hung up before anyone could answer. She kept asking herself the same questions. Why had the spot where Sister Cooper died drawn her so? Why did the girl's incomplete name reverberate in her head like the echo of a lost cry off a high cliff? What was Ms. Cooper to her? What could she be except a ghost?

Finally Jean let the number ring. He answered. She recognized his voice—she would never forget that voice.

"Hello?"

"Jim? This is Jean Rodrigues. Remember me? The girl who couldn't find the ocean?"

He hesitated. "Yes. How have you been?"

"Great. How are you?"

"Good. I finally have the place in order. You should see it. You wouldn't recognize it from the day I moved in."

"Can I see it today?" she blurted out.

He paused. "Is something wrong?"

"No. It's just, you know, I want to see you again. I had fun with you that day. I was disappointed when you didn't call." She lowered her voice, knowing she had no right to ask the question but wanting to do so anyway. "Why didn't you call?"

He took forever to answer. "The move was kind of rough for me, in a lot of ways I'd rather not go into. I didn't think I'd be very good company for anyone." He paused. "But if you want to get together that would be great."

"Would tonight be OK?"

He laughed—it sounded forced. "Sure. What time should I pick you up?"

"I'll come to your place."

"Are you sure? I don't mind driving over. I remember where you live."

"I'm sure. I think I can get my mother's car. I really do want to see your place. And that whole section of town is so much nicer than here." She added, "I feel more at home there."

CHAPTER

X

*J*EAN WAS IN JIM'S PLACE five seconds—they had hardly said hello—when she noticed Shari Cooper's picture. A four-by-five color photograph in a gold-leaf frame, it stood on his desk beside his computer. Jean had not seen it while helping Jim move. Without asking permission, she crossed the single large room of his studio apartment and picked it up. The girl was attractive with layered blond hair and longish bangs. Her face shone; her expression was intelligent. An eighteen-year-old girl with plans for the future. Her big green eyes, in particular, had depth. Yet, to Jean, the details of Shari Cooper's appearance were unimportant. It was the person behind the face that interested her. Holding the photograph, Jean's hand began to shake, and she realized that the enchanted pool that granted the mysterious visions was not only found in the deep woods. Sometimes a senior picture in an unsigned yearbook pointed the way to profound mysteries.

She knew this girl!
Like she knew the reflection in her own mirror.
"Who is this?" she asked softly.
Jim came up at her back. "My sister, Shari."
Shari. Shari Cooper.
Jean nodded, swallowed. "She has such lovely green eyes."
"But they're brown, don't you think?"
"No. They're green, definitely green. What's the matter? Are you color-blind?"
"Yes."
She turned and looked at him. "I didn't know that."
He shrugged. "You hardly know me at all." Gently he took the picture from her and set it back down on the desk. The sight of it seemed to grieve him, but she did not wonder why he kept it so close. It seemed he couldn't turn away from it now. She watched him for a long moment as he stared at his dead sister.
"What happened to her?" she asked finally.
He shook himself as if from a trance. The feeling in the room was close to déjà vu, yet different. It was as if the sorrows of yesterday and the hopes of tomorrow had slipped from their respective time frames and crossed paths in this place as she had crossed his path, seemingly by accident, without reason, and also because it was meant to be. She realized then that she loved James Cooper more than she had ever loved anyone in her life. Not as an attractive young man with whom she wanted to have a relationship. But because he had been Shari Cooper's brother. He shook his head.
"It's a long story. I'd rather not talk about it."

Jean reached out and touched his arm. "I know she was murdered."

His eyes widened. "How?"

"I went to the spot where she died."

He frowned. "Did you know Shari?"

"No. I never met her."

"Then why did you go there?"

"I don't know. I went for a walk and found myself at the spot where she hit the ground. An elderly woman happened by and explained that she had been pushed from the third-floor balcony."

"Then you know what happened. You don't need to ask me."

"No. I don't know what happened. Why was she murdered?"

Jim turned away. "I don't know why you want me to talk about these things." He sat down on the sofa and put his hands to his head as if it hurt. He chuckled unexpectedly.

"What is it?" she asked, crossing to sit beside him.

"I was just thinking of what you said. How her eyes were green, definitely green. I would tell Shari they were only brown, and she would always say what you said back to me." He looked at the floor. "For a second you reminded me of her."

Jean touched his knee. She couldn't stop herself from touching him. Deep in her chest, she craved for him to wrap his arms around her and tell her that everything was all right, finally, that the past was dead and buried and that they were both alive in a living universe. But she knew such a gesture on her part would disturb him. Yet she couldn't let it be, not without understanding what *it* was. The mystery of

Shari Cooper's murder? No, she thought, it went much deeper than that.

"You remind me of someone as well," she said.

He looked up. "Who?"

"I don't know." She shook her head. "I am not trying to be purposely confusing. I am genuinely confused."

"About what?"

"You. And your sister. And why the stain of her blood on the ground—please forgive me—drew me like some kind of magnet." She pointed toward the picture. "Why does she have her bangs in her eyes?"

"Shari liked them that way."

"I knew that. I knew that before you said it."

"But you just asked me why she wore them that way?"

"I was being facetious. Or else I was mimicking your mother. I bet your mother didn't like the way Shari wore her bangs."

"She didn't. She always wanted her to cut them." Jim stopped and drew back. "Why are we having this discussion? You said you never met Shari. Why should you care about how she wore her hair? Or for that matter, what else she did in her life?"

Jean fought to calm herself. "I'm sorry, Jim. I realize that by talking about these things I'm probably tormenting you. I assure you that is not my purpose. I'm not some weirdo who just happened to show up at your doorstep." She added sheepishly, "Even though I did just show up at your doorstep."

He eyed her cautiously. "Why did you come to my parents' house? Did the elderly woman you spoke to direct you there?"

"Not specifically. But she told me your last name. She had spoken to your father after Shari's death. I found the address in the phone book."

"So you *happened by* on purpose?"

"Yes."

"Why?"

"I told you, I don't know why. There's something about you and your sister that draws me. This morning I went to the grave of a friend. Her name was Debra Zimmerer. I do volunteer work in a hospital and she was a patient there. We didn't spend a long time together, but we were close, you know. Sometimes it doesn't take long to get to know someone. Anyway, I went to her grave to read her a story I wrote, and while I was there the thought 'I want people to remember me' popped into my mind. And then I thought of you and your sister and I felt I had to call you—and like I said, I really don't know why I am telling you all this." She paused to catch her breath. "I'll leave now if you want me to."

He was hardly listening. He was staring at the picture of his sister again. No, not at it but just to the right of it, at his computer. A great change had come over him. His face had become pale—he was ghost-like.

"Jimmy?" she said.

"She used to call me that," he whispered.

"Shari used to call you Jimmy?"

"Yes."

"I'd assume many people do."

"It's the way you say it. Just like her." He considered. "Besides being color-blind, I have a habit of walking in my sleep." He regarded her with something akin to awe. "Did you know that?"

"No. But that could be dangerous."

He nodded. "Shari always worried about me hurting myself while I was out for a nocturnal stroll." He continued to study Jean. Something she had said in her ramblings touched a nerve in him. She suspected she knew what it was. "You said you write stories?"

"Yes. A few. Why? Do you write?"

"No. I mean, I did write one story." He looked back at his computer. "While I was sleepwalking."

"Really? You were unconscious?"

"Yes."

"Wow. What was the story about?"

He drew in a breath. "My sister."

"That's nice that you'd write a story about her."

He shook his head. "No. I told you, I was asleep when I wrote it. And it wasn't exactly a story about her. It—it described what it was like for her when she died."

Jean sat stunned. "Are you serious?" Stupid question. Jim was near tears. He nodded weakly.

"I woke up one morning a few days after she died and found it in my computer. Apparently I had been up the whole night typing it in." His shoulders slumped. "That's the only explanation I have for its being there."

Jean felt cold then. Like a portion of the dark dirt of Mother Earth, a portion far beneath the surface that remained hidden as the years of man went by. A portion that was never supposed to be uncovered until the end of time. The cold was both terrifying and thrilling.

"Something I said reminded you of that story?" she said.

"Yes."

"She said in the story that she wanted to be remembered?"

"Yes. Those were her last words."

"But you wrote the story?"

Jim, Jimmy, wept then. He held his head in his hands as the tears trickled silently over his cheeks. "I don't know, Jean. I'm like you, I just don't know anything anymore."

Jean reached over and hugged him, and as she did so a wonderful glow radiated outward from her chest. The simple act of being able to comfort him meant so much to her. As if she had wanted to hold him in the past but had been unable to do so. She ran her fingers through his hair and pressed her face against his.

"I have to read that story," she whispered. "Please let me read it. If I don't I'll never know who I am."

He sniffed, embarrassed, his face damp. "But you're Jean Rodrigues."

She drew back, but continued to hold on to him. "Yes. But I don't know who *she* is. I feel like I've had two lives. At the beginning of the summer I also fell off a balcony. And since then I've been walking around in a dream. I have to wake up, Jimmy." She stared down at his hands, then let go of him and looked at her own. "I have to understand how I can now type stories I couldn't imagine before. I couldn't even write a one-page paper all the time I was in school."

"When did you fall off the balcony?"

"I don't know the exact date. It was a Friday night, two weeks before I was to graduate from high school."

"Shari died two weeks before she was supposed to graduate."

Jean looked over at the computer. It waited on his desktop like a modern Aladdin's lamp. She only had to rub the keyboard a little and the megabytes genie would appear and offer her any wish, except the wish for more wishes. But what could Shari Cooper, sitting like an angel on her brother's shoulder as he labored unconsciously in the dark, have asked for in her story except for another chance to be alive?

I want people to remember me.

Sometimes memories just weren't enough.

"Let me see it," she pleaded.

Jimmy went over to the desk and sat down and booted the computer. A menu appeared on the monitor listing files. He moved his mouse around and the computer beeped. Then he stood and offered her his chair. "It's a long story," he said. "It'll take you several hours to read. I can leave you alone until you finish it."

She stood. "You don't have to leave."

He raised a hand. "I want to. I have never let anyone read it before. I think it will be hard for me, you know, to sit here while you go through it." He wiped at his face and forced a grim smile. "I might start crying again. Guys aren't supposed to cry."

Jean stepped toward him and gave him a hug. "I'm scared, Jimmy."

"What are you scared of?" he asked, holding her.

"What happened to her. Who she was. Is her story scary?"

He let go of her. "Much of it is, yes. But much of it is beautiful as well. You'll see. I think it ends happily."

Jean glanced past him at the computer. "I'm glad."

Jimmy nodded and left her. This strange girl he hardly knew from the wrong side of town, all alone in his apartment with the most private aspect of his life. Jean wondered at his trust, but then realized he felt the same way about her that she felt about him. A love so old it must have been alive before they were born.

Jean sat down in front of the screen.

She moved the cursor. Words appeared.

Dark and disturbing and beautiful words.

Most people would probably call me a ghost. I am, after all, dead. But I don't think of myself that way. It wasn't so long ago that I was alive, you see. I was only eighteen. I had my whole life in front of me. Now I suppose you could say I have all of eternity before me. I'm not sure exactly what that means yet. I'm told everything's going to be fine. But I have to wonder what I would have done with my life, who I might have been. That's what saddens me most about dying—that I'll never know. . . .

Jean read only a small portion of the book. She didn't have to read much. Before the party began, the birthday party that would stretch over a nightmare period of events and end days later in a dreary funeral, and finally days after that culminate in another murder attempt, she knew all the characters. All their names, their likes and dislikes, all their passions and hatreds. All their secrets as well, and it was those especially that made it clear how it would end for Shari Cooper, and why it was that she did die so young. Jean, in fact, knew everything about the story. Because . . .

"I wrote it," she whispered aloud.

She remembered.

I remembered.

I, Shari Ann Cooper.

CHAPTER
XI

I FOUND THE RISHI sitting cross-legged in meditation
by the stream where I had left him. Peter was not with
me; I told him I had to have a private talk with the
Rishi, which hurt Peter's feelings a little. Peter had
become worried on the flight back from the center of
the galaxy. I wondered if he could sense my insight
into what a problem his suicide was going to be.
Quietly I sat down on my knees in front of the Rishi.
He was still wearing his blue silk robe and looked as
wise and wonderful as ever. After a minute or two he
opened his eyes.

"More questions, Shari?" he asked softly.

"Yes. Is this a good time? I don't want to disturb
you."

"No problem. What troubles you?"

"Several things. I was wondering when I would
return to a physical body?"

"In a few minutes."

"What? Why so soon?"

"Because you are ready to return now. And I don't

want you to postpone it. The more time you spend
enjoying the freedom you have on this side, the harder
it will be for you to go back. Besides, do you know
how much time has passed on the Earth you knew
since you died?"

"No."

"A year. I see your surprise. Time is not a constant
throughout the creation. It is as much a product of
consciousness as space. Here time is different. At the
center of the galaxy it is even more different."

"But I thought I would have more time to goof off
over here. I mean, there's still so much I need to learn
before I go back."

"No. You know all you need to know. Also, I will
continue to watch over you while you're on Earth. I
will guide you, have no fear." He paused and briefly
closed his eyes. "Besides, Jean Rodrigues is ready to
take her fall. I see her now. She stands on a balcony
overlooking the city much as you stood on a balcony
before you left your body. Her mind turns to God. She
prays for help." The Rishi opened his eyes and there
was much love on his face. "We have to help her."

"But there are a few things that still confuse me.
When we first talked, I assumed Peter was also talking
to someone like you, a great teacher."

"Yes. He talked to me. But he saw me in a slightly
different way and he called me Master."

"At the same time we talked?"

The Rishi smiled. "Time is time to me. It is all the
same."

"What did you tell him?"

"Many of the same things I told you. I answered his

questions. But we did not talk about Wanderers." He paused again and studied her in that gentle penetrating way he had. "I see what is in your heart, Shari. You want him to return with you."

I nodded. "Yes. Is it possible?"

"A better question would be, is it advisable?"

"You don't think it is?"

"Trust your intuition, Shari. What do you think? Or better yet, what do you feel in your heart would be best for him?"

I shrugged helplessly. "I don't know. But I sense the issue of his suicide is a problem, after all. More of a problem than I realized before we went into the light. Is that true?"

The Rishi nodded, and for once his expression was grave. "Human life is the greatest of God's gifts. Because it is only in a human nervous system that a man or woman can realize God. Even the angels in the highest heaven have to be born human to attain perfection, to become a Master. To purposely throw away such a gift is an unfortunate mistake. Don't misunderstand me—Peter is not damned because he killed himself, despite what certain religions might say. He will learn from his mistake and go forward like everyone else. It is simply that his suicide slows him down. He doesn't have all the opportunities open to him at present that you do. Naturally, though, these will be his in the future. God forgives all mistakes even before they are committed. It is important that we are able to forgive ourselves."

"But didn't Peter do that before he stepped into the light?"

"Yes. That is why he was able to follow you. You helped him in that way, as he helped you in other ways. But the consequence of his suicide will still be there when he returns to a physical body. There is a term for this—*karma*. His suicide created difficult karma for him."

"How will that karma take shape?"

"It can take a variety of shapes and forms."

"But you don't want to tell me?"

"Many of these things are up to Peter. As far as I know, he hasn't said anything about wanting to return to the physical right away."

"Because he doesn't know I have to go back. You said I am to return in a few minutes and I feel a lot of pressure. Can the three of us talk about it before I return?"

"There is no pressure, Shari. If you don't wish to go now, you may go later. It is simply that the time for the change is auspicious for you as well as Jean. But another auspicious time will arise. It always does. But certainly the three of us can sit and talk together before anything is decided. I can bring Peter here now."

"In a moment. I wanted to say that if you feel the time is ripe, then that's good enough for me. I'll go and quit whining. I really am grateful that you set this all up for me. But I wanted to ask you—how long will I be on Earth? You said I'd write stories that millions will read. Does that mean I will live to a ripe old age?"

"No. It may be that you return for only a short time. I spoke of this period of transition that is fast approaching on the physical plane. Just as many Wanderers are incarnating on Earth to help with the transition, many with negative vibrations are also returning to stop it. They will not succeed, but they can upset the plans of many men and women of good will. In particular, they dislike Wanderers and attack them when they have the chance."

I shivered at the idea. "Can they spot a Wanderer?"

"Many of them can. Many of them are highly evolved, but in a negative way. I know that sounds like a contradiction, but it is not. One can evolve either positively or negatively. The interesting thing is whichever way you choose you end up merging into the divine. The divine is all there is. But the negative path takes much longer and is no fun. There is no love on that path. Those of negative vibration crave power and dominance. That is their trademark. You can spot them that way. They try to place themselves above others. They feel they are especially chosen by God for a *great* purpose. But God chooses everybody and all his purposes are great." He paused. "One of the negative beings might kill you. It's possible."

"But can't you protect me?"

"Protect you from what? Death? There is no death. I have nothing to protect you from."

I nodded. "If they do get me, then I'll be back here with you. That won't be so bad. But I would like to help humanity as much as I can while I'm on Earth. What else can I do besides write my stories?"

"Meditate. I will guide you to a genuine Master. Do service. Service performed without the expectation of reward brings a glow and richness to life. Study people who are always helping others. They are happy. You will have a happy life even if it doesn't last forever. That is my promise to you."

I bowed my head in gratitude. "Thank you." I sat back up. "And now I suppose the hour grows late. Please have Peter come."

CHAPTER
XII

*M*Y IDENTITY CRISIS was over, even though I didn't know I'd had one to begin with. Jean Rodrigues's memories were still there as clearly as was her body, and so was I. The fusion of her life with my soul brought me no confusion. Although I could not clearly recall everything the Rishi had told me, I remembered him well and trusted that he would not have put me in a body where I didn't belong. Before I did anything, even as I stood up from Jimmy's desk, I thanked him again, as well as said a prayer for the original Jean Rodrigues. But I knew she was well because she was with him. My Master.

I turned off the computer. I could read the rest of it later.

Stepping onto the balcony that adjoined the apartment, I saw my brother sitting three stories below beside the pool and staring at the water. I remembered how I had sat beside him in the car after I died, while he drove from the morgue to the condo where I had been killed. How he had pulled off to the side of the road and wept. How I had wanted to take him in my arms and tell him everything was all right. And now God had given me that chance, I thought, and here I was crying. The pool was practically right beneath me. My tears must have been landing on his head. He looked up in my direction.

"Have you changed your mind about reading it?" he called up to me.

I shook my head.

"Has it upset you?"

I shook my head.

"Do you want me to come back up?"

I nodded.

I was sitting at his desk when he came back in, studying the picture of my past incarnation. Honestly, I couldn't decide whether I looked better then or now. One thing for sure—Jean had bigger breasts. I was glad I hadn't gone out with Jimmy and let him touch them or anything. I would have just *died.*

Now what was I supposed to do? It took me two seconds to make a decision. I had to convince him who I was. If I didn't, I knew I would spend the rest of my life regretting that I hadn't at least tried. Also, I believed the time was ripe for revelations. I believed the Rishi had moved Jimmy to let me read the story. That was why Jimmy had gotten emotional around me, something I knew he seldom did. I believed the Rishi's grace was all around.

I couldn't get over how I had been dead and was now alive.

I was so happy.

"What's wrong?" he asked quickly. "You look like you've been crying."

I set my picture down. "Yes. But that's all right. Please have a seat. I have something to tell you. You're not going to like what I say at first. You're going to get angry and order me to leave. But if you'll let me continue, then something wonderful will happen. Something beyond words."

He studied me quizzically. "What are you talking about?"

"I haven't read all of Shari's book. I don't need to. I know it from beginning to end. But I don't want to talk about particular incidents in the book. You could always say I happened to glance at a particular part and know what happened. Or else you could say I somehow got ahold of a copy and read it beforehand in order to confuse you."

He sat down on the couch. "You are confusing me. What are you talking about?"

"Jimmy, what do you think of me? I don't mean am I pretty or interesting or boring or crazy. I mean, is there something about me that you find familiar?"

He hesitated. "Yes."

"What is it?"

"I don't know."

"Do I remind you of anyone?"

He lowered his head. "No."

I understood that he was saying yes. But that it was not possible for him to say yes to his suspicion because what he suspected was not possible. Besides, the entire subject of Shari Cooper was so painful for him. I realized I'd have to punch a hole through that pain if I was to stand any chance of convincing him that I had come back from the grave. I took a deep breath. This was not going to be easy.

"I'm going to list a few events that happened between you and your sister. Only you two knew about them, no one else. None of them is discussed in her story. What I want you to do is just listen as I talk. Don't try to form any conclusions. Can you do that?"

"Yes. But you already said that you never met my sister. How can you know anything about us that isn't in the book? Have you talked to her friends? To Jo?"

"No. Even Jo wouldn't know the things I'm about to say. Please, just let me talk for a few minutes." I paused for effect. "On Shari's first day of high school she locked the number of the combination of her locker inside her locker. She was so embarrassed she didn't tell anyone what happened. But she came to you at lunchtime and asked if she could borrow some money to buy something to eat because her lunch was in the locker, too. She made you swear you wouldn't tell anyone what had happened and you kept your promise."

"No. I told my mother what had happened."

I jumped in my seat. "You told Mom? Why the hell did you do that?" I stopped myself. Nothing was sacred, I thought. "Never mind. Let me take another example. On the night of your first date with Amanda, just before you went to pick her up, you entered Shari's bedroom and asked your sister how far you should try to go with Amanda. Like should you kiss her or just hold her hand—those kinds of questions. And Shari told you with a perfectly straight face that you should try to have intercourse with her before taking her to dinner. Do you remember?"

Jimmy sat up. "Yes. How do you know that?"

I raised my hand. "Be patient. When you were

fifteen and Shari was thirteen, your parents took you for a trip to the desert. The two of you woke up early and decided to hike to a nearby rock formation. But what neither of you knew was that distances are deceptive in the desert and that the rock formation turned out to be five or six miles away. By the time you got to it you were both exhausted and thirsty. Then, on the hike back, while climbing through a dried ravine, you heard a rattlesnake in the nearby shrubs. Both of you panicked. You jumped out of the ravine and left your poor sister alone with the snake. She peed her pants. The rattlesnake looked at her and just crawled away. Afterward you both realized you had behaved like cowards, and you made a secret pact not to talk about what had happened." I paused. "You never told anyone about that incident, did you?"

"No." He was getting annoyed. "How do you know about it?"

"Let me tell you one more incident, and then I will try to explain myself. This happened after Shari died, but it is not recorded in her story. It did not happen between you and Shari but between you and Mrs. Parish. Listen closely here, it might sound a little confusing. After it became known that Amanda had killed Shari and that *she* was in fact your real sister, and not Shari, you went over to visit Mrs. Parish, Amanda's mother, who was in reality Shari's mother. While you were there you both talked about how great Shari had been. Toward the end of the conversation you made a touching comment. You said, "I think the things I loved most about Shari were all the things that made her different from me. In a way I'm grateful she wasn't my blood sister because then she wouldn't have been so different. She wouldn't have been who she was, which was the greatest sister in the world." After that you asked Mrs. Parish not to repeat the remark because you feared it would get back to your parents and they might be hurt by it."

There was a strange light in Jimmy's eyes. It was kind of scary, actually. But so is the fine line between fear and hope, pain and joy. It was as if I were being guided directly by the Rishi right then. I knew I had to take Jimmy to a place where he was about to explode before I hit him from just the right angle. I believed I was closing on that place fast.

"How do you know that?" he asked softly, his voice thick with feeling.

"Because I was there with the two of you when you spoke about Shari."

"That's impossible," he said flatly. "We were alone in her house. Amanda was under arrest at the time. How did you know about what happened in the desert?"

"Because I was there."

"I don't understand."

"In each of these incidents, I was there."

He spoke with exaggerated patience. "No, Jean. You weren't there. I would have known if you were there."

"Then how do I know these things? You explain it to me."

"I don't know. You must be lying. You must be a friend of Jo's. Shari must have told Jo these things and Jo told you."

"The phone is right there. Why don't you call Jo and ask her if she knows a Jean Rodrigues?"

His fear increased, as did his anger. "How do I even know your name is Jean Rodrigues? Why are you talking about these things? What are you doing here?"

"Do you want me to leave?"

"Yes." He stood. "As a matter of fact I do."

"Not thirty minutes ago you left me alone to read your most private computer entry. Now you're kicking me out. Sit down, Jimmy, I told you what I had to say would make you angry."

He sat back down. "I'm going to give you another three minutes."

"Good. That should be enough. If you were to call Jo, you would discover she knows no one who fits my description. If you were to call Mrs. Parish, you would learn she has never repeated your remark to anyone. Mrs. Parish is an extremely sensitive person. She would say nothing that might hurt your parents."

"So you know her at least? You're admitting that?"

I had to take another breath. "I know her in a manner of speaking. I know all of Shari's friends. I can tell you about them at length. But they do not know me. There isn't one of them who would recognize me." I paused. "Strange, isn't it?"

"Yes. If it's true, but I doubt it is."

"Why do you doubt it? Think about what I've just told you. Think about the things only you and Shari could have known."

"That's not true. Shari didn't know what I said to Mrs. Parish. She was dead at the time."

"No. That's what I'm trying to tell you. She wasn't dead. She was there in that house with the two of you!"

He stood again and pointed at the door. "I want you

to leave. I don't know who you are or what you want. I just want you out. Now."

I stood and walked toward the door. But I stopped in front of him, I had to stop. He was my brother, after all, my big brother. My Jimmy. I stopped and rested my open palm on his chest and looked up into his eyes. He didn't brush me off. He appeared to be transfixed by my touch, my eyes—there was a hint of green in them somewhere, I thought. Not that it mattered since he was color-blind. He had not been able to see the color even before I died. How could I hope that he would now? Still, I stared at him and I felt so much love for him that my own vision began to blur and he lost definition in my sight. Then I couldn't even tell what he looked like. It was then, however, that his face appeared to soften, and not just because of my tears, but perhaps because the old saying about the eyes being the windows of the soul was true. It was then he finally reached up to pull back the curtains a little. He reached up and squeezed my hand in that moment.

"Who are you?" he asked.

"It is me standing here. Just me."

"It was me lying there," he whispered, quoting from my story. "Just me." He brushed a tear off my cheek. He shook his head sadly. "It can't be you."

"I haven't forgotten you. How can you have forgotten me?"

He got choked up. "It can't be you."

I shook his hand. "Look at me! I'm here in front of you! What does it matter that my body has changed? It's still me."

He wanted to walk away, but I wouldn't let him. I

held on to his hand as if it were a lifeline to safety. His head fell forward as if dragged down by weights. His eyes blinked at the floor. His anger was all gone now. There was just pain and a ray of hope.

"But you're dead," he said pitifully.

"Was I dead when I sat beside you that night and wrote my story? Jimmy, what was that story written for? To let everyone know that death does not exist! How can you have forgotten the main point of the stupid book?"

He shook uneasily, almost talking to himself. "But I didn't write it. I was asleep. I didn't know what I was doing. I just woke up in the morning and it was there."

"I wrote it!"

"It can't be. It can't be you."

"It is me! Look at me, Jimmy! Just look and you'll see. I've come back. I came back for you."

He looked up. I had the window at my back. Perhaps the light from it reflected on his face. Perhaps an angel brushed a wing over his forehead. I don't know. All I know is the scale finally tilted between the unequal balance of his longing and his grief. Just one more grain of sand had to be placed on our side, I saw. But he had to do it, not I. He had to say it.

Master! If you really are there now, please help us.

"Shari?" Jimmy said.

"Yes." I smiled. "You remember me."

CHAPTER

XIII

*T*WO HOURS LATER we were both still talking our heads off and busting our guts laughing. And the funny thing was, it was as if I had never died. It was as if we were continuing a conversation we had started over a year ago. But the reverse was also true because it was the best talk we ever had. Sweeter than any I could remember. Neither of us would have come up for air if Jimmy hadn't suddenly begun to look tired. I commented on the fact and he shrugged.

"I've been working a lot of overtime lately," he said.

"For the telephone company? Still chopping down those telephone poles?"

He shook his head. "Is there nothing you don't know about me?"

"I'm sorry, but this Chicana babe remembers everything about her big brother." I reached over and felt his head. "I also remember you have diabetes. I think you need your insulin."

He nodded. "You're probably right. You know that

was always one thing that amazed me about you. You knew when I needed a shot before I did."

"That's because I'm not color-blind, and I can see when you start to turn green."

"Do I look that bad?"

"No. I'm exaggerating. Are you still taking ten units in the afternoon?"

He stood and shook his head and stepped toward the bathroom. "I had to increase my dosage after you died. The doctor said stress has that effect on diabetics. I've never been able to bring it back down." He glanced back at me. He was obviously tired but hadn't lost his smile. "It just struck me how odd it sounds to talk to someone about her own death."

"I got used to it on the other side with Peter."

"That's right, good old Peter Nichols." Jimmy stepped into the bathroom and opened his medicine cabinet. "He didn't happen to wander back into a body, did he?"

I hesitated, feeling a lump in my throat. "No. He's still—gone."

Jimmy noticed my tone. "But you know he's fine where he is?"   .

I nodded. "But you can know one thing with your head and feel something quite different with your heart. I miss him."

Jimmy pulled out a short strip of paper he used to test the blood sugar level of his urine. He closed the door only partway. The simple act meant a lot to me. He felt comfortable enough with me that he didn't have to close the door completely.

"You'll meet plenty of guys with those tits," he said casually.

I had to chuckle, although the topic made me a little sad. "To tell you the truth I already have a boyfriend. I inherited him from Jean. His name's Lenny Mandez."

"How do you feel about him?"

The question caught me off guard. So did my own answer; it just popped out of my mouth. "I love him," I said.

"Interesting," Jimmy remarked from the other side of the door.

"It is." I had to ask myself why I loved Lenny. He wasn't exactly Shari Cooper's type, not by about ten light-years. There was no question in my mind I had a distinct identity separate from the one Jean had formed over her eighteen years on Earth. Yet I had her memories; they were as much a part of me as they had been of her. When I sat quietly, it was easy to understand how someone like Malcolm X had not been able to pierce through the memory barrier. If not for meeting Jimmy and reading my own book, I doubted if I would have been able to do it. I realized so much of our identity was tied to our bodies, and wrongly, because we were much more than that. Still, the allure of the flesh was strong. I could close my eyes and feel exactly how Jean had felt on her first day of high school—she had been stoned, naturally—and what it had been like to make love to Lenny for the first time. The latter experience had been more satisfying than my one roll in the hay with Daniel. Lenny, at least, knew what it took to please a girl.

Or he used to know, I reminded myself.

I had to see him soon. I missed him.

"Damn," I heard Jimmy mutter.

"Did you pee on your hand?" I asked.

"That's a personal question if I ever heard one."

I giggled. "I'm glad you're testing your sugar level and not *estimating* like Amanda advised that night."

He popped his head out of the bathroom door. "You were there that night?"

"Of course I was there. You read that in the book. I saved your life, brother."

He shook his head again. "I have no doubt you're Shari, but it's still taking me time to absorb it all." He paused. "What did you see that night?"

"Are you asking if I saw the two of you screwing?"

"I never did it with Amanda."

"Gimme a break. When I got to our house that night the two of you were wearing bathrobes and nothing else."

"We didn't do anything."

"Yeah, right, sure. Why are you embarrassed to admit it? Is it because she turned out to be your sister?"

"Reread your own book, Shari. You will see we *definitely* did not have sex. Besides, what about you and Daniel?"

"I never did it with Daniel."

"Sure you did. It's in your book."

I was dumbfounded. "I put that in my book? God, you're right. You know I only wrote that because I was dead at the time. We've got to take that out."

"We've got to take out the part about Amanda and me. Even though we didn't do anything."

"No. We can't do that."

"Why not?"

"It's a major plot point. Daniel—he was just a

minor character. The story doesn't revolve around whether I had sex with him or not."

Jimmy was worried. "You're not thinking of trying to get that story published?"

"I have to get it published. It's part of my mission on earth. To enlighten humanity about profound spiritual matters."

"But you can't publish that story."

"Don't worry, Jimmy. We can tone down things between you and Amanda."

"No. That story can't go out in that form. Mom and Dad will hear about it."

"Is that so bad? I want them to read it. I want to go see them next."

Jimmy came back into the room and sat on the couch beside me. "You can't tell Mom and Dad who you are. They'll never believe you, no matter how many personal incidents you recount. You'll just end up hurting them."

"But my being dead hurts them."

"That's true. But it's been a year, Shari. They're getting over it. I know that must be hard to hear, but it's true. If you show up at their doorstep and say you're their daughter and a Wanderer—they'll freak. You know them. They'll never accept it."

"But you accepted it."

"Because we were very close. I can see beyond your body. Also, I have always been open to metaphysical ideas. Mom and Dad aren't. The only esoteric thing they do is read their horoscopes in the paper every now and then."

I sighed, knowing he was right. It was a painful

realization. One of the first things I thought of when my memory had returned was to go see my parents and ease their grief. I had imagined all kinds of beautiful scenarios. Now I had to forget them.

"But can't I at least go over and see them?" I asked. "As a friend of yours?"

"Yes. But you'll have to be careful what you say."

"You never showed them my story?"

"No."

I nodded reluctantly. "Maybe that was wise. But I do want to try to get it published. I can always change the names and places."

"That's a good idea. We'll do that."

I hugged him. "You're so wise and yet I'm the one who's supposed to write the stories. Is it possible we could work together?"

"Only if I get half the royalties."

"No way! You're as bad as Sam."

"Who's Sam?"

"He's my muse. He's a troll and lives in my closet in South Central."

Jimmy's eyes widened. "Are you serious?"

I socked him. "You idiot! You still believe everything I tell you. Just because I came back from the dead doesn't mean there are trolls. Anyway, have you given yourself your insulin? I want to go out."

"Yes. Where do you want to go?"

"I want to see Jo and Mrs. Parish, my real mom. I want to see Detective Garrett, the guy who investigated my murder, as well. Boy, do I owe him. I hope he hasn't started drinking again. I'm telling Jo who I am. She'll believe me. She was practically born on the back side of a Ouija board."

Jimmy nodded. "We can see Jo. She lives on the other side of town. She's going to U.C.L.A."

"I was going to go to U.C.L.A."

"You can still go."

"My grades aren't good enough. Jean Rodrigues spent too much time in high school smoking dope. And I doubt U.C.L.A. will accept a transcript of Shari Cooper's grades on an entrance application. Besides, I don't have the money to go there. I live in the ghetto."

"We can change that. Tomorrow, you can move in here with me."

I stopped to think of the Rishi's words. My memory of my time with him was fragmented. I wondered if it was because we had spoken in a place outside of normal time. I knew he had told me to write and serve and meditate. But there were other things I sensed I had lost upon returning to the physical. He had given me some kind of warning—

"No," I said. "I have to stay with my new family. It's important that I work in that area of town to help improve things. Anyway, I never cared that much for material things." I paused again. "But I would like my Ferrari back."

"Who doesn't care about material things?"

"Well, it was mine. Where is it?"

"Dad sold it."

"*My* car? Who did he sell it to?"

"Your old boyfriend."

"Daniel is driving *my* car?"

Jimmy laughed. "It gets worse. He's still going out with Beth Palmones."

I waved my hand. "I don't care about that. He tried to make it with her an hour after my funeral. They deserve each other. But it pisses me off that he has *my* car. Could you buy it back from him?"

"That car cost a hundred grand. I don't have that kind of money. Besides, you can't drive a Ferrari and live in the ghetto. It wouldn't last a night there."

"The ghetto is not as bad as rich white kids like you think. It has a lot of color. Take my best friend, Carol, for example. She's full of life. I have to introduce you to her. Maybe you two would hit it off." I paused. "Maybe not."

"Why do you say it like that?"

"Because she's a lesbian." I giggled. "But for a guy who's slept with his own sister, a lesbian might be a step in the right direction."

Jimmy was beet red. "Would you drop that? You know that's not true. Besides, I didn't know she was my sister. I thought you were my sister."

I quieted in a hurry. "You do still think of me as your sister, don't you? I still think of you as my brother. The fact that Amanda and I were switched at birth doesn't mean that much to you, does it?"

"Don't worry. You will always be my sister."

I was relieved. "Good."

"But there is something I think you should worry about. Should you see Mrs. Parish so soon after recovering your memory?"

"I'm not going to try to convince her who I am."

"I realize that. But she's a sensitive woman. She might sense something unusual about you and it might upset her. You might get upset around her."

I shook my head. "You forget, I have walked through the valley of the shadow of death. I am much stronger than when you last said goodbye to me. I don't mind getting upset. And Mrs. Parish is wise. If she does notice something about me, she'll be able to assimilate it in her own way. She doesn't have to understand that I'm Shari, but she can know that I am someone close."

"You want to see her now?"

"Yes. Please take me over. It means a lot to me."

He considered, then nodded. "That woman is an angel, as well as your mother. I suppose it's only right you should see her."

CHAPTER

XIV

I HAD A PECULIAR EXPERIENCE as Jimmy drove me up to Mrs. Parish's place, a small apartment over someone's garage. She had moved since I'd last been on Earth. I thought of Mrs. Parish not in terms of how I remembered her, but how I had written about her in my story. My memory of my life as Shari Cooper, I realized, although distinct, also was blank in a few spots. I was Shari but someone else as well, and I wasn't just talking about Jean Rodrigues again. It was like I was a third person, a new and improved version of the other two girls. But the memories I had from after I died, the ones I could recall, didn't suffer from this veil, and perhaps that was the reason I thought of Mrs. Parish the way I did.

Mrs. Parish had an arthritic spine. Often, if we were alone in the house, she would let me help her sweep the floor or scrub the bathrooms. . . . Her hair was not one of her finer features. It was terribly thin. Her scalp showed a little, particularly on the top, whenever she bent over, and she was only fifty. To be quite frank, she

*wasn't what anyone would have called a handsome
lady. She did, however, have a gentle, lovely smile.*
Mrs. Parish smiled as she answered the door. Her
right leg was encased in a walking cast. Her hands
were covered with liver spots. She had lost consider-
able weight, and seemed more stooped, older than
fifty-one. But her smile was lovely; it made my heart
leap in my chest to see her.

"Jimmy," she said. "What a wonderful surprise.
And you've brought a friend." She offered her hand.
"Hello, I'm Mrs. Parish."

I shook her frail fingers. "I'm Jean Rodrigues."

Mrs. Parish stepped aside. "Please come in. I was
just making myself coffee. Would you like some? I
know Jimmy does. Black with cream, right? I have
carrot cake as well, but I know Jimmy doesn't want
any of that."

"The coffee would be great," Jimmy said. "Jean
drinks it as well. How did you break your leg?"

"I was cleaning a friend of your mother's house,"
Mrs. Parish said as she limped into the tiny kitchen.
There wasn't room to watch MTV in the apartment,
but I supposed she didn't need much space now that
Amanda was away in a state psychiatric hospital. Mrs.
Parish opened the refrigerator and continued. "I was
mopping the woman's floor when I just slipped and
fell. I lay there for three hours before anyone came
home. I couldn't even get to the phone. Have a seat,
Jean, Jimmy, make yourselves at home."

"You poor dear," I said, sitting down.

Mrs. Parish chuckled. "It was my own fault. I'm
getting clumsy. Anyway, I've been stuck in here for a
couple of months. And the doctors say it will be

another two months before I can go back to work."
She finished putting on more coffee and came over
and sat down near us. "Oh, well, at least I have a
chance to catch up on my reading."

"I read a lot," I said. "I write stories as well."

Mrs. Parish was interested. "Do you now? That's
wonderful, to be able to put your ideas down on
paper. You must let me read your work. I'm sure I'll
love it."

"I would be flattered to have you read it."

Mrs. Parish gestured to Jimmy. "So how did you
two meet?" she asked.

"I knew his sister," I said quickly.

Mrs. Parish blinked. "Did you now? Shari?"

"Yes," I said, holding her eye, with Jimmy staring at
me, fidgeting, no doubt wondering what I was up to.
"I was one of her best friends. I only learned a short
time ago that you were her actual mom. I told him I
had to meet you."

Mrs. Parish had to take a breath. "I'm sorry, Jean, I
never heard Shari talk about you. But it's always nice
to meet someone who knew her. Did you two go to
school together?"

"No. I live on the other side of town. But we often
talked on the phone."

Mrs. Parish nodded pleasantly, but her face fell a
little. "She was a lovely girl."

I leaned forward. "Another reason I wanted to meet
you is because I wanted to share with you an experience I had a few days after Shari died. I thought that
you would be the one person who could understand it.
But if it's too upsetting to talk about her, I understand."

She straightened. "No. Please tell me. I want to hear."

I thought of what Mrs. Parish had said to the empty air as I sat beside her in the days after I died.

"Shari. If you're there, if you can hear me, I want to tell you something that I almost told you a thousand times while you were alive. Finding you again after losing you for all those years was wonderful. It was the best thing that ever happened to me. It brought me so much joy, I thought I would never ask God for anything else, because he had given me everything. And I kept that promise, until right now. You see, I have to ask him one more thing, to tell you this, that I loved you as much as any mother loved a child. You were always my daughter."

"I was sitting alone in my living room and thinking about Shari," I said. "There was no one at home, and somehow I dozed off in my chair. I had this dream that Shari was with a woman about your age and she was helping her sweep a floor. The woman had a sore back, and when Shari set her broom down, she rubbed the woman's spine to ease her pain. She said to her, 'Mom, finding you again was the most wonderful thing that ever happened to me. I know how much you loved me. Don't worry about me, I'm fine. I just wanted you to know how much I loved you. When I was alive, deep inside, a part of me always knew you were my mother.'" I paused. "Then something woke me up. A hand on my arm. But there was no one there, Mrs. Parish." I spoke gently. "Does my dream mean anything to you?"

A soft light shone on Mrs. Parish's face. In that moment, even with her wrinkles and her cast and her liver spots, she reminded me of the Rishi. They both had grace.

"Yes," she said quietly. "It means everything to me. Thank you, Jean, for sharing it with me." She touched her chest. "I know in my heart she's all right."

I stood and went over to hug her. I was crying again—for maybe the tenth time that day. A baby cried when it was born, and for me this was like my birthday. It felt so good to hug my mother again.

"I know she is, too," I said.

CHAPTER
XV

*W*HEN WE GOT BACK to Jimmy's place, I asked if I could call my mother. Jimmy did a double take. "Jean Rodrigues's mother," I explained. "She'll be worried about me."

"You never used to ask if you could use my phone. Maybe you aren't really Shari. Maybe this is all just an elaborate hoax."

I picked up the phone. "I asked you once out of politeness, but I'm not going to ask you again."

"Oh, *that* sounds familiar. I guess you are Shari, after all."

I smiled at him. "Behave yourself. There are other secrets I can put in my book that will ruin your reputation." I punched out the number quickly. My mother, Mrs. Rodrigues, answered. I felt as close to her as I had the day before. That was the great thing about having two sets of memories. Overnight I had doubled my family. The only drawback was that I could think of twice as many people who annoyed me.

"Hello?"

"Hi, *Mamá,* it's me. I'm safe and sound. Haven't keeled over from any bad headaches. I'm with a friend in Orange County. I might be out late. Just wanted you to know. How are you doing?"

"I'm fine but Carol is upset. She's called three times. She wants you to call her immediately."

"Qué pasa?"

"I don't know. She wouldn't tell me. But whatever it is, I don't want you getting involved. You hear me?"

"Yes. Is she at home?"

"I think so. Who is this friend you're with?"

"He's an old pal. I'll tell you about him later. I want to go. I want to call Carol."

"Remember what I said," she warned.

I hung up the receiver and quickly dialed Carol. Jimmy watched me. "Do you still get headaches as a result of your fall?" he asked.

"Yes, and they're a real bitch. But don't worry, I'm not going to die on you again." Carol picked up. I turned my back on Jimmy and shielded the phone with my hand. "Hello, baby doll. What's the big emergency?"

Carol sounded agitated. "I got bad news. Darlene's got herself a piece. Freddy told me she bought it from a crack dealer on Hawthorne."

"That's no big surprise. We knew she was shopping."

"Yeah. But here's the scary part. Lenny checked out of rehab and went straight to Darlene's house. Freddy told me that, too. Maybe Darlene got the piece for Lenny. I hear he can drive. You hear what I'm saying?"

"That he might try a drive-by on Juan and take the heat?"

"Yeah. You better talk to him. Better talk to him now."

"I'm on my way. *Gracias.*"

"Take care of yourself, Jean. I have a bad feeling about this."

"I'll call you as soon as I know something."

Jimmy was studying me when I set the phone down. I forced a smile.

"I have to go," I said. "A problem at home."

"You don't want me to get Jo? You were so excited about seeing her a minute ago."

"You can get her. I might be able to come over later." I edged toward the door. "I'll call you."

He stepped in front of me. "What was that remark you made about someone doing a drive-by and taking the heat?"

I laughed. "Oh, that's just tough girl talk. It's nothing."

He crossed his arms over his chest. "I'm not stupid, Shari."

I stopped laughing. "It's nothing to worry about, Jimmy, I promise. I'll be back in two hours. Go get Jo. Tell her what's happened. I bet you can convince her even without me there. I might be back here before you. Leave the door open for me."

"Can't I go with you?"

"No, and I can't explain why. The situation is complicated."

He stepped aside reluctantly. "Why do I feel like I did the last time we said goodbye?"

"Will you be out late?"

189

"Not too late."

"Good."

"What's the matter?"

"Nothing. I'm just tired. Have fun."

"Sweet dreams, brother."

"Take care, sister."

I went up on my tiptoes and kissed him on the forehead. "I will not be out late. I will come back. Trust me, I love you too much to leave you again."

"Love can't protect you from everything, Shari."

I opened his door. Outside, it was beginning to get dark.

"There's nothing I need to be protected from," I said.

Darlene Sanchez's house was a pile of old wood, plaster, and bad vibes. Her father had abused her when she was six. When she was ten he had taken two rounds in the chest from a double-barreled shotgun while trying to rob a liquor store. When she was sixteen her mother died from cirrhosis of the liver from having drunk half a liquor store. Darlene was tough, though, I knew from past life regressions. She could take a few setbacks and come out shooting. That was what worried me.

Darlene answered the door when I knocked.

"Jean," she said. "What are you doing here?"

"Is that how you say hello?"

"Hello already. What the hell are you doing here?"

"I want to see Lenny."

"He's not here."

"I don't believe you." I pushed at the screen door. "Let me in."

She pushed back; she was a strong devil. "No. I'm with a guy."

"You're with *my* guy. Open the goddamn door or I'll come in through the window."

Darlene was dark. "I wouldn't recommend that, Jean."

I laughed in her face. "What are you going to do, shoot me? Do you feel empowered because you bought yourself a piece today? Yeah, I heard about your gold credit card purchase. Do you think owning a gun makes you bad? You make me sick. You prance around like you're so hot to avenge your boyfriend's death, and then when it comes crunch time you drag a crippled guy into your stupid plot and tell him to do all the dirty work."

"I don't know what you're talking about."

"I'm sure you don't." I suddenly shoved hard on the door, catching her by surprise. I was inside before she could stop me. Lenny, in a wheelchair, sat beside the kitchen table. He glanced over as Darlene started to grab my hair.

"Let me talk to her alone," he said flatly.

Darlene stopped with her hand in the air. "Alone?" she asked, annoyed.

"Yeah," Lenny said. "Go for a walk."

"This is *mi casa!*"

"Go for a long walk," Lenny said.

Darlene went for a walk. I went over and sat at the table near Lenny. Physically, he looked better than when he had transferred from the hospital to the rehabilitation clinic, which was the last time I had seen him. He had some color and had put on weight. But his handsome face was still flat and cold. I felt as if

I were about to talk to a perfect stranger. I'm sure the original Jean would have felt the same way. He offered me a cigarette, but I shook my head. The air was thick with smoke already. He took a puff on his own cigarette butt and ground it out in a filthy ashtray.

"You look good," I lied.

"For a cripple?"

"I'm sorry, I didn't know you would hear that when I said it. I'm glad to see you're up and around. What is it like handling the chair? I bet it takes some getting used to."

He snorted. "It's like riding a bicycle. The only difference is the ride never ends." He added softly, "Unless you decide to crash."

"You don't want to crash. You've come too far. Lenny, look at me. Talk to me. You're doing good. Ten weeks ago you were lying in a hospital bed. Now you're able to go places and see people. This is a fresh start for you. It can be a fresh start for us. I care about you—a great deal." I stopped and asked sadly, "Don't you care about me?"

He finally looked at me. "You look different."

I forced a smile. "Is that good?"

"I don't know." His eyes narrowed. "What have you been doing lately?"

"Waiting for you to call. But other than that I've been busy. I start school in a couple of weeks. I'm going to the JC. I've been working at the Subway and at the hospital." I added, "I've written a few stories. You can read them if you'd like."

He shrugged. "I never read. Why did you come here tonight?"

"I just told you. To see you. I'm worried about you."

He smiled thinly, as he had when Jean told him she was pregnant. "You don't have to worry," he muttered, leaning back in his chair and stretching. It seemed as if he had a cramp in his back.

"Are you all right?"

"Yeah. I just broke my back is all."

"Lenny!"

He shook his head. "I don't know why you're here."

I sat back, suddenly as tired as the whole sick house. "I heard Darlene bought a gun. I heard she wants you to kill Juan for what he did to Sporty. I'm here to talk you out of it."

He chuckled. "You know nothing."

I stood. The air in the house was too heavy. Reason could not prevail in such an atmosphere, I thought. I had to get him somewhere else. "Let's go for a ride," I said.

"To where?"

"A friend's house."

"Who is this friend?"

"It's a guy I met. You'll like him. Let's go before the dragon lady gets back."

He surprised me. I thought I would have to drag him out the door.

"If you want," he said.

Jimmy's third-story apartment had an elevator as well as a stairway. The former had proved most useful when I had helped him move in, although the elevator had not been wide enough to accommodate his bed and chest of drawers. Fortunately, Lenny and his wheelchair fit in the elevator nicely, and soon we were rolling into Jimmy's apartment. The place was empty.

"Does he usually go out and leave his place unlocked?" Lenny asked.

"This is Orange County, not South Central," I said.

"They know what the word *crime* means over here. Do you have a key to this guy's place or what? How well do you know him?"

"I know him very well. But he's not my boyfriend or anything like that."

Lenny gave a bitter laugh. "Like I'm supposed to believe that. Like you're going to wait for me to get better when you know I won't. Drop the charade, Jean. You're screwing this guy. We both know it."

My temper flared. Maybe it was about time. Maybe it was the worst time. Time, I knew, was different in Orange County than it was in South Central. As it was different on Earth than at the center of the galaxy. What had I seen there? That we were all part of one another? If that was so, then Lenny had just become an aching head that I just wanted to rub softly or else pound furiously. I just wanted the madness to stop.

What I did not know was that he wanted the same thing.

"You drop the charade, you bastard," I said. "I am not screwing anybody and you know it."

I was very surprised when he pulled a black revolver, complete with silencer, from underneath his shirt and pointed it in my direction. His grin was the work of demons.

"Oh, I know a thing or two about you," he said. "I

know you were screwing Sporty when you were supposedly going out with me. I know it was his baby you got pregnant with. And I know that you're going to die in the next two minutes."

I held out my hands defensively. I may have walked through the valley of the shadow of death and come back out again, but that didn't mean I was anxious to repeat the experience on a nice summer evening. His words had shocked me so much that I actually smiled instead of screamed. But it was an awkward smile, full of pain and fear. Yeah, it hurt me that he would even point a gun in my direction, my boyfriend. Of course, I knew it would hurt a lot more if he pulled the trigger.

"Hold on just a second," I said. "I never slept with Sporty. What gave you that idea? I was certainly never pregnant with his baby. You got it all wrong. Who have you been talking to?"

"I don't need to talk to no one. Last spring I drove by your house late one night and saw you kissing Sporty goodbye. It was kind of dark but what you gave him was no brotherly peck."

Frantically, I tried to remember that night, searching memories that not only didn't belong to me, but in more cases than not had been recorded with a stoned nervous system. There was one time, in mid-May, when I did recall that Sporty had been over late. He and Jean had been smoking pot and goofing off. She might have kissed him good night—he was an old friend of hers—but I had no recollection that it had been a hard kiss. The problem was, Jean might have been so high she momentarily thought she was necking with Lenny and went at it a bit. What a paradox, I thought. How could I defend myself for things she might have done? But one thing for sure, I knew Jean had never slept with Sporty.

"I might have kissed him, I can't remember," I said quickly. "We were high that night. But I didn't sleep with him. You have no proof of that."

He sneered. "No proof? You told me you were pregnant. You *were* pregnant. You lost the baby in the fall. You told me that as well."

"So? It was your baby."

"It couldn't have been my baby! What kind of fool do you take me for? I wore a condom every time we had sex."

I chuckled despite the situation. "You are a fool. The condom broke once. You didn't even notice, but I did. That's how I got pregnant with your kid."

"You expect me to believe that?"

"It's the truth. It happens all the time. Ask any doctor or pharmacist. They'll tell you the same thing."

My words seemed to shake him. The gun in his hand moved off to one side. But I didn't think to try to rush him and wrestle it away. Lenny was six feet away, and even with his injury I knew he had excellent reflexes. If I jumped him, I'd die, it was that simple. And I would have lied to my brother a second time.

"It can't be," he whispered, more to himself. His face went gray; his very soul seemed to tremble. "Sporty had to go."

"What did you say?"

He regained control of his aim. "You're a lying, cheating bitch. That's all there is to it. I'm going to kill you now. Move over onto that balcony."

"No! I heard what you just said. You were the one who arranged Sporty's death. You took him into Juan's territory that night. What did you do, tell him that you had arranged a truce for him with Juan?"

Lenny was enraged. "I didn't shoot him! I didn't pull the trigger!"

"But you set him up. I see it all. I should have seen it a long time ago. You told Juan where you'd be walking by and at what time. No wonder you didn't get hit. No one was aiming for you. And you call me a cheat. You grew up with Sporty, for chrissakes!"

"And he was screwing my woman! He deserved to die!" Tears sprung into his eyes as he glared at me with the dark hint of murderous guilt. It was then I understood, even before he said what he did next, that he felt he had to kill me to justify what he had done to his friend. To convince himself that he had not made a mistake. It was twisted logic, and unfortunately it was the kind practiced daily in the barrios every time some innocent person died.

"No one deserves to die so young," I said.

"I didn't want him to die! It was you who made him die! It was you and your goddamn slutty ways! Get out on that balcony. I tried to kill you once—knocking you off my balcony—and by God I'm going to do it this time. Get out there, you bitch!"

He was serious, there was no arguing with him. I stepped out onto the balcony, not taking my eyes off him. He followed me only partway. The wooden balcony was cramped, the sliding glass door that led to it even more narrow. He might be able to wheel his chair out, I thought, but it was obvious he didn't want to. The night air closed around me like a hand of doom. I couldn't comprehend that my time back on Earth was to be so short. Was my karma so bad? It didn't seem fair. The Rishi hadn't warned me.

Yet he had, I thought, in a way.

"What happened that night, Lenny? Did you set the balcony to collapse beneath me? At the critical moment, did your handiwork fail? Did you climb down beneath me to fix it and then—big surprise—me and the balcony fell on you? You know, you always were lousy at fixing things."

"Cállate!"

By his reaction I knew I had hit the bull's-eye. "Just tell me if Darlene was in on your little escapade."

"She wasn't."

"Great. That's a relief. Now what? This balcony isn't going to collapse beneath me, and I'm not going to jump off it. I've had enough of that stunt."

Lenny smiled grimly. "But you are going to jump. The pain is going to make you jump."

"What pain?"

Wrong question. Lenny took aim and fired.

The bullet burst from the muzzle in a silent flare of orange light. It tore through the right side of my right thigh with an agonizing red rupture. Even when I had hit the concrete with my head after falling three stories, I hadn't felt such overwhelming pain. Crying, I sagged to the side and instinctively covered the wound with my right hand. The blood poured warm and sticky into my palm. It soaked my pants and dripped onto the boards of the balcony. Lenny shifted the gun and aimed it at my left thigh. Where were Jimmy's neighbors? Watching cable TV? I had to scream, I knew, to get their attention. But I also knew if I did, he would just put a bullet through my heart. Oh, God, I thought. I should never have come back.

"You should jump now," he said. "I will take you apart piece by little piece. A few more bullets and the pain will become intolerable."

"You'll never get away with it," I gasped. "The police will come. They'll catch you. You'll go to jail forever."

My threat amused him. "Your new boyfriend will probably get here before the police. I'll do him like I'm doing you, slowly and painfully. I have plenty of ammunition. I'll save a bullet for myself. When the police get here, there will be no one to arrest." He put pressure on the trigger. "Would you like it in the crotch? You can cover the area with your hand if you like, but the bullet will go right through it and get you where it hurts most."

"Please." I wept, holding out my trembling arm, horrified at the thought of what it would be like to be shot there. "Give me a second. I'll get up on the railing. I'll do what you ask. I'll jump."

He was happy. He was sick. He was like some ancient beast dug up from a black tomb that the gods should have long ago covered with a sacred mountain. His eyes shone the color of blood, and I hardly recognized him.

"That's a good little slut." He cackled. "But do it fast, my finger is itchy. Dive headfirst if you don't want me to shoot at you while you're lying splattered on the concrete."

"I'm hurrying," I moaned, easing myself up onto the wooden railing. All I could think was that I couldn't let him put another bullet in me. From so many violent films and TV shows people have become anaesthetized to what it is like to be shot. It is a tragic thing. My lives were tragic. They kept bringing me to a precipice where there was no hope of escape. I eased my bloody leg over the railing. "Lenny," I pleaded, before I let go.

He was not there, not the guy I knew. But the gun was. It pointed through the railings at my crotch. "You have two seconds," he said. "One—"

I let go, partly. My hands slid down the wooden railings and I was left hanging on to the floor of the balcony. My legs dangled below me; it felt as if a river of blood dripped out of my torn thigh. The pain was already intolerable, and my plan was really no plan at all. My only hope was that now that I was below his line of vision, he wouldn't be able to shoot me, not without wheeling out onto the balcony, which I prayed was too narrow for his chair.

Unfortunately, my status as a Wanderer did not make it inevitable that God would take my prayers under consideration. Peeking up over the side of the balcony, I saw Lenny approach steadily, past the coffee table and through the sliding glass door. His big round black wheels coasted to the tips of my fingertips. It was there he aimed the gun, not at my head. He must have had some deep-seated perverse wish to see me fall. I swore if I did, I would let out a scream so loud everybody would come running. Before my brother could come running. A scream was the one thing I had failed to let out the last time I had died, and as a result most people thought I committed suicide. Of course, that would not be a problem this time with the bullet hole in my leg.

"One," Lenny repeated.

"Jesus, Lenny."

"Two."

He fired at my right hand. My fingers were sprayed; the bullet splintered the wood between them. Technically, he didn't hit me, but the shock of the striking bullet was enough to make me lose my grip with that hand. Careening wildly to the left side, I fought to bring my right hand back up onto the balcony. It was a loser's strategy. So what if I got it back up. He would just shoot my fingers off, and there would be that much less of me to bury.

Still, I fought.

Still, I could not comprehend that this was really happening to me.

Not again. Lenny's wild face loomed above me.

"Master!" I cried.

Lenny's face suddenly softened. "Shari," he said, as if surprised.

Time could have halted. I stared at him.

"What?" I said.

He reached down to save me. I reached up.

But he was too late. I lost my grip. I fell.

I saw the edge of the apartment roof, the stars. There were only a few of the latter, and they weren't very bright. Not compared to the lamppost that stood near the entrance of the apartment complex, which suddenly began to rush toward me at an incredible speed. I had been this route before. I knew how the stars would change when my head hit the ground and I rolled over and looked up. There would be millions of them in the sky then. Orange ones and green ones and blue ones. There would especially be red ones, which would multiply rapidly and blot out everything else in the heavens as a colossal wave of smothering hot wax—all the blood in my brain—ran out and covered my face.

I would black out. I would die.

CHAPTER
XVI

*W*E SAT IN A TRIANGLE. Peter looked uneasy. I didn't feel so hot myself, not for being in heaven. The Rishi, however, had lost none of his equanimity. The clear stream trickled nearby. The air was still fresh with the fragrance of flowers. The sun shone; in this realm it seemed never to set. I wondered if Peter saw the Master as I did, but I supposed it didn't matter. I only hoped that Peter listened to him.

"What's going on?" Peter asked.

"I'm going back now," I said.

"To where?" Peter asked.

"Earth. A physical body. But I'm not going to be born as a baby. I'm going to enter the body of an eighteen-year-old girl named Jean Rodrigues. I'm going to be what is called a Wanderer."

Peter's face sagged. "You're going to leave? You can't leave. We just got here." He appealed to the Rishi. "What's the big rush?"

"There are reasons," the Rishi said calmly.

Peter was distraught. "But I don't want her to leave. Shari, don't you have any say in this?"

"I do. It's all up to me. But I have to go. Not just for myself but for other people as well. I have something important to do on Earth."

"But won't you miss me?" he asked pitifully.

My eyes moistened. "Yes."

Peter turned to the Rishi. "Can I go with her? I have to go back if she's going."

The Rishi considered. "It is possible. But I wouldn't advise it. You have much to learn on this side, Peter, before you return. The last time you were in a physical body, you made some mistakes. If you return too quickly, you might repeat the same mistakes."

Peter was taken back. "Are you referring to my suicide?" he asked quietly.

"Yes," the Rishi said.

"But I won't do it again. Especially if I'm with Shari. I'll know how foolish an act it was."

"When we return this way," I said gently. "We don't necessarily remember the spiritual realm. The Rishi, the Master, has explained how easy it is to get caught up in matter again."

"The chance to become a Wanderer is a great gift," the Rishi agreed. "But it is also a huge responsibility. You would be more ready to accept that responsibility if you spent more time between lives."

Peter would not listen. "But I don't want to be here if she's not here. I—I love her. You told me when I arrived that the main thing in creation was love. Don't my feelings count for something in this decision?"

The Rishi smiled faintly. "They do. Divine love transcends all reason. It is the path to God. But is your love divine, Peter? Or do you wish to return simply because you will miss her?"

Peter was stubborn. "My love for Shari is as real as my love for God. I know that. You're so wise—you must know that."

The Rishi gestured innocently. "I know that I don't know. That is how I can feel the will of God." He briefly closed his eyes. "I feel many things right now. If you go back, it will be hard for you."

"I don't care," Peter said. "As long as I'm with Shari. Can you promise me that much at least?"

The Rishi regarded Peter gravely. "Yes. I can promise you that. But you threw away your last life. When you steered your motorcycle in front of the truck, you almost lived. Had you survived, you would have been crippled for life. If you return now, you will return as a cripple."

"No!" I cried. "That's too horrible. There must be another way."

"Those are the choices," the Rishi said. "It is up to Peter to chose."

"Don't do it," I said to Peter. "You know me, I live recklessly. I won't be gone so long. Stay here and learn what you have to learn. You don't want to be in a crippled body. You might not be able to have sex."

Peter smiled sadly. "But I would rather have love than sex. I would rather have you than have legs that work." He reached over and took my hand. "Even back in our bodies, you won't forget me and I won't forget you. It can work, I know it." He added, "If that's what you want, Shari?"

"I don't want you to spend years suffering."

"I won't suffer if you're with me."

I smiled through my tears. "What are you talking about? I'll drive you crazy."

"I enjoy being crazy about you," Peter said. He appealed once more to the Rishi. "Can I go? I accept that I will have to be crippled. I see the justice in it."

The Rishi nodded. "You may go."

I was still worried. "But is this the best course?"

The Rishi laughed easily. "I must confess this entire conversation has been something of a test for both of you. Everything I said about the reasons you should stay were true, Peter. But I love love more than anything in this creation. Don't worry, Shari. If someone makes a sacrifice in love, then only good can come from it in the long run. Good will come from Peter's decision, for both of you."

"Is there anything we can do on Earth to help us remember this time with you?" Peter asked.

"Shari has asked me this question several times," the Rishi said. "My answer to you is not the same. For you to remember, Peter, you will need a huge shock. You will have to return to that moment of despair that previously made you take your life. You will have to face it squarely. And this time you will have to decide to live." He paused. "What did you think of just before you died?"

Peter considered. "I thought of Shari."

The Rishi nodded and stood. "Then events will arrange themselves so that the lesson is repeated. I hope you pass the test. But if you don't, you will just have to take it again later." He offered both his hands, one for each of us. "Come children, it's time. Lenny and Jean are in the hospital, unconscious."

EPILOGUE

WHEN LENNY AND I had entered the apartment complex, we had, as I said, used the elevator because of his wheelchair. The lift was at the front of the complex. The pool was in the rear. Lenny, therefore— probably not until he wheeled himself out onto the balcony to try to shoot off my fingers—did not even know there was a fair-size body of water almost directly beneath the balcony. There was another important element in the scenario. Just before I lost my grip, as I fought to reach for Lenny's hand, I swung up with my right arm. The move was in one sense counterproductive and in another sense beneficial. It had the effect of making me lose my grip, but it also threw me away from the balcony and farther out over the central courtyard, just before I started on my long fall to my death. Yet I didn't die.

To make a long story short, I landed in the deep end of the swimming pool.

Boy, that was one bellyflop that stung.

I bobbled to the surface ready to scream. The water

was already stained with my blood. Just then Jimmy and Jo came by. Jimmy took one look at me and appeared ready to faint. But Jo burst out laughing.

"Hey, Jimmy," she said. "You are right. That must be Shari. She's still jumping off balconies." Jo walked to the edge of the pool and offered me a helping hand. "If you are Shari, then I finally have a nickname for you."

I let Jo pull me out of the pool. My leg hurt something awful, but as long as it didn't have to be amputated, I didn't mind. I remembered that Jo often gave people nicknames. I noticed that she had bleached her hair blond. She always did want to have more fun.

"What's that?" I asked my old friend.

She giggled. "The *Fall Girl.*"

"Shari!" someone called from three stories up. "Are you all right?"

"Yeah! Is that you, Peter?"

"This is turning out to be a weird day," Jimmy muttered.

"Yeah!" Peter shouted. "I remember! I remember you!"

I smiled. "That's what I wanted most!"

TO BE CONTINUED . . .

About the Author

CHRISTOPHER PIKE was born in Brooklyn, New York, but grew up in Los Angeles, where he lives to this day. Prior to becoming a writer, he worked in a factory, painted houses, and programmed computers. His hobbies include astronomy, meditating, running, playing with his nieces and nephews, and making sure his books are prominently displayed in local bookstores. He is the author of *Last Act, Spellbound, Gimme a Kiss, Remember Me, Scavenger Hunt, Final Friends* 1, 2, and 3, *Fall into Darkness, See You Later, Witch, Die Softly, Bury Me Deep, Whisper of Death, Chain Letter 2: The Ancient Evil, Master of Murder, Monster, Road to Nowhere, The Eternal Enemy, The Immortal, The Wicked Heart,* and *The Midnight Club, The Last Vampire,* and *Remember Me 2: The Return,* all available from Archway Paperbacks. *Slumber Party, Weekend, Chain Letter,* and *Sati*—an adult novel about a very unusual lady—are also by Mr. Pike.